Charles Heathcote has al
very rarely leaves. A Crea
Cheshire, Charles is the a
novels about Mrs Doris
is the first in a series of cosy crime novels to feature
Alice Valentine and Marmaduke Featherstone.

Also Available

Our Doris
Indisputably Doris
Doris Ahoy

To Chris

Thanks for all the
"steamy" conversations.

An Heir to Murder
Charles Heathcote

Best Wishes

Charles Heathcote

VA
VARIOUS ALTITUDES
Cheshire

Chapter One

Alice wished she'd never laid eyes on Mrs Sylvia Cameron. There had been some mix up with the paperwork and as such, rather than spend Thursday afternoons helping the impoverished of Partridge Grove she found herself assigned to a ninety-three-year-old woman with an acid tongue.

It didn't last long.

Alice chose to take the high road and signed Sylvia up for a tea dance.

Unfortunately, Alice made a mistake. A mistake that cost her a job, her reputation, and, to some extent, her fashion sense.

She recalled her manager's face at their final meeting. He looked like a bewildered owl as he said, 'Can you tell me what was going through your mind when you sent a nonagenarian to a Zumba class, Alice?'

She hated meetings. She'd considered blaming her error on the recent death of her Aunty Magdalena but that felt too dirty, and thus she told him the truth. She said, 'I won't lie. I typed in "Thursday tea dance" and booked the first thing I saw. I never thought Google would go with key words over common sense.'

Alice had never seen someone so disappointed in her and she once had to tell a boy that French kissing didn't involve *pain au chocolat*. Her manager, Keith, straightened his tie, coughed a cough that sounded as though he were checking the strength of his own prostate and said to Alice, 'I have to say I thought you could have made something of yourself here. Instead, you've allowed one mistake to ruin your entire career.'

Alice couldn't help herself. She felt the old glimmer of mischief catch in her throat like a hastily swallowed pear drop. Before she could stop herself, she said, 'You're the one ruining my career, Keith. You could have put me under supervision, demoted me, left me making coffee for Mary Hinds with the prosthetic leg, but instead you're allowing this smear campaign by Mrs Cameron's family to decide for you. You've about as much integrity as gluten-free bread.'

'It was a Zumba class.'

'Many older women enjoy Zumba.'

'At ninety-three?'

'There's no upper age limit, they don't discriminate.'

'She died.'

'Well, is it really that much of a loss?'

Keith gave her until three o'clock to clear out her things. Not that she had many. She could have broken all manner of data protection laws, stole client details and sold them off to cold callers. She didn't. She didn't even take her mug because when she got to the kitchen Mary Hinds was using it and Alice wasn't sure she could take something from a woman who lost her leg on an exercise bike.

Instead, Alice left with just her coat and handbag, and a few dozen paperclips, a stapler, an ergonomic keyboard, and the keys to Keith's Mazda. Keys she helpfully dropped down the nearest grid.

Alice did what any twenty-five-year-old with a free afternoon would do; she went to see her mother. Or rather, she went to the pub and was in the middle of a large Pinot Grigio when her mother walked in, followed by a whole host of Nordic walkers.

Primrose Valentine was never one to shy away from maternal duties. After taking one look at Alice she ordered a bottle and joined her daughter, as did the posse of Nordic walkers and their poles, looking like a group of tourists who'd dismantled a garden fence.

Alice swigged the wine like medicine, gulped hard, and said, 'Aren't you going to introduce me?'

Primrose, in the midst of escaping from her Craghoppers jacket, said, 'Just give me a second, love, you know I never got the hang of waterproofs.'

'You might want to try taking your rucksack off first.'

'What rucksack?' Primrose looked at Alice the way only a mother can when she senses their child is making fun of her.

Alice quirked an eyebrow, the lower half of her face hidden behind her glass.

Primrose cocked her head to the side. She groped her body as though performing her very own security check and stopped still, her hands on the clasp of her rucksack. Her eyes went wide for a moment before she said, 'That's one of the many wonders of modern clothing. There's no weight to it. I swear I could fit seventy tins of baked beans inside and walk to Tunstall with little complaint.'

'Really, Mum?'

'Well maybe not Tunstall, but I'd get far.' Free of her

waterproofs, Primrose sat down across from Alice and said, 'Now, how is my beautiful daughter?'

Alice necked the last of her wine. 'I've been sacked, Mum.'

'Well, I guess I'll be buying lunch then.' She reached for the menus as the landlady appeared with their drinks.

They remained quiet for a few minutes. The Nordic walkers talked amongst themselves as Primrose allowed the silence to build. Alice knew what she was doing. Her mother would never ask what happened in case she was being too intrusive, something that would ruin her reputation as a modern mother who allowed their child space to form their own opinions about the world. This strategy worked perfectly well when Alice was seven and too naïve to keep secrets, but as soon as she hit puberty it became a problem. When Alice broke up with her first boyfriend, Primrose didn't speak to her for three weeks, and even then Alice only gave in because her father offered her twenty quid.

Alice would eventually tell her mother, but for now she said, 'What's with the Nordic walking?'

Primrose shot Alice a look of mild astonishment and said, 'I think I'll have the halloumi, how about you?'

'Because you're already a member of so many clubs and societies. Does Dad ever get to see you?'

'You've always been the same. Steak and chips. No thought to the welfare of the animal as long as you've eight ounces of prime rump in your mouth.'

'Says the woman who can't even go for a walk without her hand around a pole.'

'I'll have you know there are two.'

Alice snorted. 'Who's a game girl, then?'

They laughed, leaving the Nordic walkers to look at

them somewhat stupefied. Primrose met Alice's gaze as she poured the drinks. 'I'll go and order, shall I?'

There was a lump in Alice's throat that she didn't want to admit to. She'd spent years training to be a social worker and she'd thrown it all away because she was too impatient to thoroughly check a webpage.

Alice said, 'I will tell you at some point, Mum, I promise.'

'I don't doubt you will, Al, we're not in the business of keeping secrets.' Primrose headed towards the bar to place their order.

A vole of a man leant towards Alice and said, 'I hope you don't mind me saying but you and Primrose have an interesting relationship. Has it always been like that?'

'Was this her first session?' Alice asked.

'Well, not exactly. There are taster sessions and training sessions before they'll even let you join the walks.'

'That's interesting.'

'It is?'

'Yes. You see, my mother has so many different classes on the go. I'm surprised she's stuck with it so long.'

'That's Nordic walking for you. It gets you out into the countryside, and then you have the poles – well, that's just like having a full-body workout, which you appreciate after sixty-seven, I can tell you, and we usually stop at the pub afterwards, supporting the local business and all that.'

Alice hadn't expected the man to stop chatting. He was definitely more of a rambler than a walker. She allowed his words to sink in before saying, 'And you are?'

They shook hands. His handshake was as limp as a

dead haddock as he said, 'Arnold. I'm the group's leader.'

'Oh, leave off, Arnie, she's young enough to be your granddaughter,' one of the women called.

'Great-granddaughter in this day and age,' said another.

'You're not wrong there, Eunice,' said the first. 'Our Chardonnay says as there's a girl in her class expecting a child at the same time as her grandmother.'

Alice gulped back some more wine to silence herself. She knew the case, had been involved at one point, and despite some lack of education in the merits of condoms, they were a good family.

She'd always hated how quick the public were to make judgements about private lives, and although she knew they came from a place of ignorance rather than intolerance, she always found it difficult to hold her tongue.

Primrose returned to the table as the walkers began to talk amongst themselves again. 'I forgot to say, it's your Aunty Magdalena's will reading tomorrow – will you be there?'

Alice's eyes ballooned in their sockets. 'How come you're only telling me now?'

Primrose shrugged.

'You must have known this weeks ago.'

'I did,' said Primrose, elongating the words so that she sounded like the winding down of an air raid siren. 'I meant to tell you, Alice, but it kept slipping my mind.'

'Why didn't Dad tell me? She's his aunty.'

'You know what your father's like. Ever since he got that new helmet-cam, he's thought of nothing else. Sometimes I think he'd have paid me more attention if I'd been a bike.'

'No doubt he would.'

Once more they erupted with laughter, earning looks from the walkers. Alice didn't blame them; even she didn't feel too much like laughing. She was twenty-five, jobless, and living with her parents. She'd become the type of person the Daily Mirror warned against. She almost considered buying a badge that proclaimed her a millennial and making the best out of a bad job.

Soon after, their food arrived. Apparently, the Nordic walkers hadn't got the message that Primrose and Alice would be dining, and had no choice but to watch them eat, marvelling at the way that Alice, a relatively slim woman by anyone's standards, could attack a steak. Arnold even went so far as to comment that she looked like a lioness devouring a buffalo. When she offered him an onion ring he soon shut up.

With lunch finished, Alice and Primrose left. Rather, Alice's father came to pick them up as they'd become so inebriated that their breath would likely boil the tarmac on the roads.

Norman Valentine had seen his wife and daughter in worse situations, and as he followed the familiar routine of lifting and packing, he wondered just why all the women in his family were completely off their trees.

It had been a long while since Alice had been drunk during the day. She usually only allowed herself the opportunity on Christmas Day, and birthdays, and New Year's Day, and those days when she wanted to do little more than hide on the sofa, watching reruns of Don't Tell the Bride.

She knew her father had brought her and Primrose home without incident, and remembered being put to bed, but after that she must've fallen asleep.

At six o'clock in the evening, Alice became aware of a figure looming at the end of her bed, a shadow rising like some great witch in a bad horror flick.

Alice pushed her covers back with a groan. She switched on her lamp, and as she waited for her eyes to adjust, she said, 'What do you want, Mum?'

Primrose cradled a cup of green tea as though it were a newborn and said, 'Nordic walking is a perfectly legitimate form of exercise.'

'Did you honestly wake me up to tell me that?'

'You weren't sleeping. I can tell because you were breathing.'

'And I don't breathe otherwise?'

'You know what I mean, love. Everyone's breathing slows down when they're sleeping. How else do you think I can always tell when your father's avoiding taking out the bins?'

'It's called routine. He hates taking the bins out.'

If getting drunk during the day was bad, then sobering up was worse. Alice felt like someone had split her head open and made an omelette from her brain. She pinched the bridge of her nose, squeezing hard as though all the alcohol were hidden in her sinuses. If she slept for the next fortnight, she doubted the headache would disappear. She doubted her mother would either, so she said, 'What is it you wanted to tell me about Nordic walking?'

Primrose stood drinking her tea, completely oblivious to anything Alice had said. She stared intently at the scuffed remains of a Looney Tunes sticker on Alice's wardrobe. There was a twinge of concern behind her eyes. They were slightly wide, and Alice wondered whether her mother was on the verge of reuniting with her lunch.

Alice allowed Primrose a few more moments of mindless reverie before saying, 'Mum, I know that you're upset about the state of Bugs Bunny, but I've had the sticker since I was five. It was bound to get ruined.'

Still, Primrose seemed lost. Alice watched as her mother came back to herself, her eyelashes fluttering as fast as a thousand moths let loose in a library. She kept her eyes averted when she spoke, 'Have you been on Facebook today?'

Alice sat up. 'No, why?'

Primrose wasn't supposed to be the serious parent. Primrose was the one who once held a sit-in at the high school until the governors agreed to put guava on the lunch menu. She didn't even like guava.

And now she was being serious.

Alice scrutinised her mother further. She'd changed since they'd got home. Gone were the waterproofs, replaced with her harem pants in a William Morris pattern, a grey pyjama top, and a cream cardigan so thick it could've been made from the wool of an entire flock of sheep. These were her Mum clothes. Primrose had read about the idea in 1997 and kept a supply of clothes intended to give the impression of a calming influence ever since.

Alice didn't feel calm. She tried to breathe slowly, but her lungs worked against her. Clenching bunches of her blanket, she said, 'Tell me what's wrong.'

Primrose's eyes pooled with tears, heavy trickles drizzling into her green tea. 'It's in the newspapers, Alice, I didn't know what to do.'

'What is?'

'I know how you lost your job. The woman's family went to the papers.'

'Which papers?'

'The Wren's Lea Reporter, The Partridge Mews Gazette, and the Congleton Chronicle.'

'Only there? That's hardly international.'

'It's gone viral.'

A cold cage of terror slammed around Alice's skull. She threw her covers back and sat on the edge of her bed. Not only did the room tilt as though she were trying to wander across a waltzer, but she suddenly felt restless with no idea where to put her energies. Nausea had nothing on the dread settling in her stomach.

'What do they say?' she asked.

'It's not good, love. This Mrs Cameron has a very upset family. They're saying you sent her to a Zumba class.'

Alice nodded. 'I thought I was sending her to a tea dance for the over-fifties.'

Primrose slurped her green tea. 'Her family say as you knowingly sent her in the hopes she'd die because you never got on.'

'She was a complete nuisance! She once refused me entry into the house, and had her son-in-law waiting around the corner. She'd convinced him I was a stalker.'

'Don't get me wrong, I know you wouldn't go out of your way to hurt anyone, but that does sound like a reason for revenge.'

Alice couldn't help glaring at her mother. 'I didn't have her killed. She was ninety-three and didn't take her angina medication before she left the house.'

'I wouldn't want to think she killed herself to spite you.'

'I wouldn't be surprised. She didn't have to take part in the class.' She didn't. It still made no sense to Alice that Mrs Cameron — a woman who needed an inhaler just to climb the stairs – would walk into a church hall filled with sprightly younger women in exercise gear and choose to participate. She'd been wearing a wool skirt. It wasn't what people usually wore when building up a sweat to Bruno Mars.

Alice knew there was nothing she could do about it. If she'd paid more attention Mrs Cameron would still be around to annoy her. Now she'd haunt Alice for the rest of her life. It really was difficult to think that Mrs Cameron hadn't died out of spite.

Chapter Two

The next day, Alice and her parents went to the solicitors for Aunty Magdalena's will hearing.

Aunty Magdalena was Alice's favourite aunty. She was her grandfather's sister and had always had a wild streak about her that some said was the result of her mother eating too many liquorice torpedoes whilst pregnant.

Many stories circulated about town. Magdalena once sold a ton of potatoes to a Russian spy in exchange for his silence. Magdalena's third husband was actually a Hindu princess in disguise. Magdalena never shopped at the Co-Op.

Yes, Aunty Magdalena had certainly been formidable.

After a few hiccups, Aunty Magdalena had upped sticks and emigrated with her sixth husband. They clicked in Lidl over cut-price roast ham, and the rest was history. It also helped that he was forty years her junior. Within three months they were married, and on their merry way to a new life in Madeira.

Now she was dead, and Alice wasn't quite sure how she felt.

Of course, she'd been sad. When her parents told her the news, she'd felt a great presence disappear, and it wasn't just because Aunty Magdalena weighed twenty-three stone. The thought of her not being a plane journey away left Alice feeling somewhat empty.

It felt strange not to have a funeral. Alice pleaded with her parents, but Aunty Magdalena had requested cremation. Ideally in the United Kingdom, but it couldn't be done, leaving Alice to wonder whether she'd ever find any shred of closure.

The solicitors' offices were in the centre of Partridge Mews. It was near enough that Alice had to walk down the high street receiving all manner of glares, taunts, and loud whispers. One woman asked how much Alice charged, as she'd got an uncle she wanted offing.

Alice despaired as they walked up the steps to the offices. 'All these people are going to think I'm actually a killer – off to discuss things with my brief.'

Her father put his arm around her shoulder. 'They'll think nothing of the sort. Sooner or later, someone will have a jam crisis and you'll be yesterday's news.'

Alice leant her head against Norman's chest and breathed in the familiar scent of his aftershave. Norman Valentine was the very definition of reliable. Once he found something he liked, he stuck to it, hence the reason he'd used the same brand of aftershave since 1987. Alice had bought him something different for Christmas when she was fifteen and filled with the pride of a new wage packet. Norman never wore the scent, and eventually regifted it to his boss a few years later. Norman liked to avoid disappointment, and he'd never been disappointed by Brut.

The offices were imposing. Although all efforts had been made to ensure the building looked bright and inviting, it didn't. A former Georgian townhouse with three storeys, the white walls showed no signs of the brickwork beneath and the dark green window frames exuded a sense of sickliness, or moss. Yet Alice couldn't help feeling, as she and her family entered, that she was stepping foot into a horror movie, and not one of the good ones where it's all been a dream.

The interior looked how one would expect it to look – bad art on the walls, potted plants in the corners, and dark laminate flooring throughout. Someone had taken their time to make the place look decidedly bleak.

They entered the foyer.

To their right, a young woman – practically a child, that baby-faced Alice wondered if she'd escaped from a crèche – sat at the reception desk, fielding a nuisance caller on the telephone. The receptionist nodded an apology to the Valentines and said down the phone, 'I understand your concerns, Mr Sterling. As I told you, I expected a phone call. However, Mr Murgatroyd says as you are not allowed to see the files, and he categorically refuses to represent you in future.'

As the receptionist continued with her phone call, Norman led Primrose and Alice into the waiting room.

Alice tried to catch the shock before it showed in her eyes, but they may as well have been floodlights. The sudden intake of breath didn't do much to help matters either.

If things seemed bleak before, they were definitely worse now.

They sat on the leather sofas, hard plastic chairs, even the coffee table, whose old magazines now littered the floor: the rest of the Valentine clan.

The other Valentines glowered at Alice and her parents.

Aunty Magdalena's parents had a dozen children, who in turn went on to have their own children, of which Norman was one. Alice couldn't blame her great-grandparents, really. There wasn't much doing in their day. Television hadn't been invented when they started reproducing and, with declarations of war here, there, and everywhere, spouses had to work hard to get it in whilst they could.

Although Aunty Magdalena and her siblings got on their entire lives, the same couldn't be said of their offspring. Valentine funerals were events to be splendored in Partridge Mews, as every relative strove to exude the impression that they were the most caring. This came before the inevitable brawl at the wake due to past arguments, new alliances, and that one time Roger borrowed Nigel's electric whisk and didn't return it for thirty-seven years. Their brawls had become so expected that The Harrington kept police on standby for any event involving Alice's extended family.

Norman was the first to speak. He said, 'How've you been, Roger? It's been a while.'

'What's that supposed to mean?'

'Just that I haven't seen you around.'

'Well I've been busy, haven't I?' Roger glared at Norman. He sprawled in his seat, his legs looking as though they belonged to a crushed moth. 'Busy' for Roger usually meant prison. He'd spent that much time in Strangeways that he celebrated both the birth and the 21st birthday of his son in the relatives' room. The security officer baked a cake.

Primrose ferried Alice and Norman over to the wall. An uneasy tension filled the room. Alice felt the weight of anger tickle her chest at the thought of sharing the same air as Roger and his brood.

She didn't get much chance to act on her feelings though, as the solicitor called them through. At least that had been the plan. Apparently, thirty people won't fit in an office the size of a postage stamp. As such, only Magdalena's immediate family – or their representatives – could enter.

Alice and Primrose were left in the waiting room, alongside a menagerie of other Valentines. Norman had gone to hear the will, and he wasn't happy about the prospect.

No one could be quite sure just where the animosity between the various branches of the Valentine family tree had started. They just all agreed it was there.

Thus, the silence continued.

After a few minutes, raised voices were heard from the solicitor's office. 'Alice?!'

Alice perked up and looked at the door. The voices were unintelligible, but she was certain she heard her name. Surely, she'd have been asked inside if she'd been left anything.

The office door was thrown open and slammed against the wall with all the ferocity of Mike Tyson with a speeding ticket.

Roger stood there, eyes wild, staring straight at Alice, like a hyena after a fresh haunch of zebra. The fury practically rolled off him in waves. 'You think you're smart, don't you?'

Alice stood up to face him, only for Primrose to step in front of her. 'What are you talking about?' Alice asked, somewhat embarrassed by her human shield.

'Yeah, Rog, what's she done now?' This came from another of Norman's cousins. Maybe Tiffany. She was blonde in any case.

'You want to know what she's done? What Alice, the

fuddy-duddy social worker has gone and done?'

'I know I would,' said Alice.

Roger laughed a snide chuckle. 'Don't play the fool. You're not that young.'

'If you keep offending my daughter, we'll have a problem here, Roger,' Primrose said.

'Fine. Be an idiot, I don't care.' Roger faced the room, looking every inch the town crier as he declared, 'So we're in there talking to Mr Murgatroyd, and he's telling us that Aunty Magdalena had done the noble thing and split her money fairly to all her immediate relatives. Isn't that right, Mr Murgatroyd?'

Mr Murgatroyd stood in his doorway, trembling like an ant under a magnifying glass as he nodded the affirmative. 'That's right,' he said. 'It amounts to around fifty pounds each.'

Roger shook his head. 'Fifty pounds, he says. Now, I don't know much about no money. I'm not here for that. I do know, however, that our Aunty Magdalena buried six husbands – all loaded.'

'You've still not said what any of this has to do with me.'

'You just want to gloat. Don't worry, Alice, you'll get your chance in a minute.'

'Hurry up, Rog – I don't want to miss my McMuffin.'

'Fine. Fine! Mr Murgatroyd was all set to send us on our way as I says to him, "You're missing out something very important there." And he actually had to ask me what, and so I says to him, I says, "The house." And I hope you don't mind my saying but you looked completely gormless, Mr Murgatroyd.'

'No, not at all, Mr Valentine.'

Roger clearly thought the solicitor was finished, only

for Mr Murgatroyd to continue, 'But as I said, Ms. Valentine signed the house over to Alice seven years ago. None of you have a claim to it.'

This was the wrong thing to say.

Roger tensed up, his shirt practically straining at the seams as he spun around and advanced on Alice. Spit flew from his mouth as he yelled, 'Spend your life conning old ladies, do you? We see about Mrs doo-dah and think nowt of it, but our aunty? Maybe we should speak to the police about this, you stupid, money-grabbing snob.'

Alice had no choice.

She punched him.

Alice hit Roger so hard that he fell against an umbrella stand and crushed it under his forehead. 'I'm not a snob. I didn't kill Mrs Cameron, and I had no idea about this house thing. If you don't like it, tough. I spent every spare moment with Aunty Magdalena when I was younger, and we didn't see any of you there.' Alice turned on the rest of the Valentines before saying, 'You want to talk about money-grabbing? Ask Roger about his mother's wedding ring.'

Alice grabbed her bag and left. Her knuckles hurt and she felt exhausted.

She didn't get far.

The restless energy that made her want to walk to Bournemouth and back dissipated too quickly. As soon as Alice stepped outside, the subtle warmth of May touched her cheeks, and all drive fled her body. She walked down the steps at a snail's pace, her shoulders slumped, eyes on the pavement.

A great clattering sounded behind her. 'Alice,' her father called.

She turned to see him struggling with his coat. His

arm was stuck somewhere between his sleeve and his breast pocket. Alice took pity on him. Once he no longer looked like he was fighting an invisible tailor, Alice said, 'Do I really own Aunty Magdalena's house?'

Norman nodded. 'Do you remember her asking you to sign some papers a few years back?'

'You need to be more specific than that, Norman,' Primrose said. 'Your aunty had Alice signing more papers than I don't know what.'

'Well, I knew nothing about it.'

'Of course, you didn't, love. There was no need for you to be involved.'

Norman bristled at this and said, 'Right, we're going to Mavis's for some breakfast. It'll be too busy for anyone to hear us.'

Chapter Three

Mavis Thistlethwaite didn't plan to retire. It was a well-known fact in Wren's Lea that she planned to keep her café running until the day she died, and even then they weren't too sure.

She was a short, thin spidery sort of woman who had kept her business where many others had failed, through sheer determination, and the wherewithal to battle would-be businessmen who thought they could treat her like their grandmother to win her over.

The Valentines had been regular patrons of Mrs Thistlethwaite's Old English Tea Room since its inception – not because they wouldn't try anywhere else, but because once a person set foot in Mavis's it was more than their life was worth to dine elsewhere. Indeed, when Norman's father chose to dine at a chain coffee shop in the seventies, Mavis and her cousin began a campaign in the Wren's Lea Reporter imploring folk to support local businesses lest their town be lost beneath a sea of common brands. They cited Norman's father and that was it – Alice's grandparents stuck with Mavis.

Until they moved to Whitby, in any case. Now,

Norman, Primrose and Alice had no choice but to frequent the place in their stead.

Alice supposed Mavis's wasn't too bad. There were definitely worse eateries in town. It had only been a year since an Alsatian was found dead in the freezer of the local pie shop.

Alice and her parents arrived to see Mavis having something of a heated discussion with Arthur, one of her assistants. Mr Arthur Sterling had been Aunty Magdalena's neighbour – he'd always had a lemon sherbet or three for Alice. She'd never seen him angry before, except for when his grandson accidentally mowed over an ornamental tortoise.

The Valentines found a table and became as invested as three people could in A5 laminated menus. The other customers had similar ideas as the argument drowned out the sound of Ken Bruce.

'I'm saying this for your benefit, Arthur. You need to give it up,' Mavis said, a growl in her words as though she'd consumed a hellhound.

'I can't. I appreciate what you're trying to do, but this is my fight.'

'You are a complete idiot.'

Arthur didn't reply. The two of them stood behind the counter, allowing the awkward silence to settle amongst the scones and shortbread.

'Look, Arthur, when your Ethel died she thought you might do something like this. Why don't you go up and see your Bertie?'

'You know I can't,' he said, drawling like a petulant teenager, 'I need to get down to the library.'

'To do more research, I suppose? I'll be having words with that Bill Newton – it's not right for a seventy-year-old man to be nosing around so much.'

'It's not right, is it?'

'Now Arthur -'

'I'll tell you what isn't right, Mavis — a man being killed and his murderer running free. I'm supposing it doesn't matter to you though, because he never set foot in this common, plebeian greasy spoon you call a café.'

Mavis raged. Her perm seemed to rise from her head like a furious bichon frise. 'I'd watch what I were saying if I were you. This is the premier catering establishment in Wren's Lea, as well you know, Arthur Sterling. How you dare to come in here and insult me beggars belief. Did it somehow slip your mind that I'm one of the only friends you have left? You've driven everyone away with your constant badgering.'

'I'm investigating a murder.'

'Nobody cares that some toff was killed at the big house years ago.'

'I care.'

'You care because you were supposed to protect him. Is that what stings, Arthur? That you were in charge and some fool got in the way? That you were outsmarted? That maybe you realised you were an incompetent young man and now you're trying to fix things when any normal man accepts their mistakes, confident they matured and mended their way. But you didn't, did you, Arthur?'

'Well, let me make this clear. You are no longer welcome here. You'll not be able to harass my customers anymore, and I have to say I'm glad. If you so much as look at my specials board, I'll show you the right end of a serving tray. Now, get out.'

Once again, silence filled the café. Ordinarily, diners could expect a pleasant dining experience at real oak tables; instead, they'd been faced by a slanging match so fierce that they almost reached the heights of Herbert Kettlewell and his Ivy when she discovered he'd taped over Deirdre Rachid's trial.

Alice was amazed Mavis didn't throw her cakes at Mr Sterling. She certainly never allowed anyone to insult the tea-room before.

Arthur looked like an orphaned lamb as he removed his apron. He moved slowly, his fingers trembling at the strings. He was so shocked his skin was almost as pale as his hair. He took a navy woollen jacket off a hook behind the counter and made his way towards the door with almost mechanical steps, each heel-to-toe pronounced as he walked.

He had his hand on the door handle when Mavis said, 'One more thing, Arthur. Your Ethel would be ashamed.'

He didn't reply, didn't look back, had seemingly resigned himself to the fact that his bridges weren't merely burned, they'd been incinerated.

After this, the café began to calm down. The customers chatted amongst themselves and Ken Bruce was left to get on with Popmaster.

Mavis busied herself wiping a few stray crumbs from the counter.

An argument between two old-aged pensioners didn't really suit the ambience Mavis had tried to create. Whilst the menus were typed and laminated there was still a vintage air about the place – starched tablecloths, net curtains, and, everywhere one looked, doilies. It was an homage to the social niceties Mavis had been raised on; each doily had its place and that place was often on top of another doily.

'This is *not* a greasy spoon,' Mavis said, slamming a tray against the counter.

'Of course it isn't, Mave,' said an older chap who'd seemingly attacked his toasted teacake with a chainsaw.

'Just look at the walls – you wouldn't find Dulux's finest pastel blue in a greasy spoon. It's all black and white checks with congealed gravy.'

'And you always have fresh flowers.'

'They're plastic, Mick.' She sighed. 'I don't know why I let him bother me. I know he's gone a bit funny lately, but he's grieving.'

'That may be so, but you were right in what you told him. There are folk who are getting fed up with his mithering.'

'He'll be had for harassment yet,' said a young woman who was nursing a latte. Her friends nodded in agreement.

'I hope that's all he gets.' Mavis took a pen and paper from her pinafore pocket and approached the Valentines. 'I'm sorry about that, bet you weren't expecting dinner and a show, I should charge you extra. Now, what will it be?'

They placed their orders and Mavis scuttled off behind the counter once more.

'Out twice in as many days,' Primrose said. 'People will think we've won the lottery.'

'People will think we've done well out of Aunty Magdalena is what they'll think,' Alice said.

'Let them think what they like, Alice. You can't go through life worrying about what other people think.'

Alice exchanged a glance with her father, knowing smiles alighting on their faces. Norman patted Primrose on the shoulder and said, 'That may be the most hypocritical thing you've ever said, Prim.'

Primrose's wide eyes darted from her husband to her daughter. She huffed breaths and stammered as she tried to figure out what to say. Her shoulders slumped. She sighed and said, 'You're not wrong, love, but that doesn't mean it isn't good advice.'

'It's great advice, Mum, but we all know about Lucinda Winthrop and the table mats.'

Primrose conceded. 'I know. I just want better for you, Al. I don't want you surfing the net at three in the morning trying to find the perfect accompaniment to crayfish and Michael Bolton.'

'I think you mean cure, dear.'

Norman and Alice chuckled together as Mavis approached with a tray. 'I've a latte for Alice, an Americano for Norman, and green tea for Primrose who clearly doesn't care about her mental wellbeing.'

'Nice to hear you haven't changed, Mrs Thistlethwaite,' Primrose said.

'I believe it's my duty as a hostess to make guests aware of the possible risks associated with certain consumables.'

'And what are the risks associated with green tea?'

'Boredom, irritability, and a certain sense of missing out on a decent beverage.' When she saw Primrose's incredulous expression, she went on, 'I know it's trendy to drink foul-tasting liquids nowadays – I was one of the first in line for Cup-a-Soup – but green tea? You may as well drink cat pee and call it quits.'

'If you feel so strongly about it, why put it on the menu?'

'I've got to keep up with the times, Primrose. You've got your gluten-free, your fat-free, and your fun-free. Besides green tea costs five pence a bag, and some silly so-and-so will pay me £1.75 for mossy hot water. I'll just get your food.'

'Did she just call me a silly so-and-so?' Primrose

asked once Mavis was back in the kitchen.

'She did, Mum.'

'It must be "pick on Primrose" day.' She took the lid off the teapot and proceeded to lift and dip her teabag into the hot water, eyes laser-focused on the tendril of string attached to the handle.

Alice and Norman watched Primrose before sharing another look. 'Are you okay, Mum?'

Primrose dipped the teabag and looked back at them both. 'I'm fine, love, just practising my mindfulness techniques to fully immerse myself in my green tea.'

Norman chuckled. 'That'd be a tight squeeze, it's only Royal Doulton.'

Primrose shook her head. 'Honestly. You know what I meant Norman.'

'And were you able to fully immerse yourself in your cup?' Alice asked.

'As a matter of fact, yes. I realised that Mavis has a point about green tea – it does have an acquired taste – but I do enjoy the benefits. At my age, I have to take care of myself.'

'I once saw you eat an entire chocolate cake, whilst drunk, after we had a Chinese for tea.'

'Lord knows I had fun when I was younger.'

'You're fifty-three.'

'Yes, and when I was younger I had a long-standing relationship with cheese fondue.' Primrose shook herself from an almost-reverie of dairy delights and said, 'Anyway, we've wittered on long enough, let's talk about the house.'

'All right then,' Alice said. 'How come I own Aunty Magdalena's house?'

'She made a deed of gift for your eighteenth birthday,' Norman replied.

'And didn't tell me about it.'

'No, she told you.'

'Remember, love? We called round before her life drawing class. She asked you to sign some papers.'

'And when you asked what the papers were for, she told you she was giving you her house.'

Alice's skin went pale.

Her body felt too hot, as though she'd just stepped into a bath with no cold water. She'd thought Aunty Magdalena was joking. They'd all sat in the garden and drank some of Mrs Pemberton's elderflower wine. Alice thought they were celebrating her birthday, not her first step onto the property ladder.

Aunty Magdalena said she'd remain in the house until Alice decided she needed space away from her parents. As Alice stayed there so often, it only seemed right that she should have the house.

And Alice thought it all a joke, that it was nothing more than a dream to infuriate the assorted descendants of Magdalena's siblings. She recalled tipsily signing paperwork, certain that Aunty Magdalena was on the verge of senility.

'You should tell someone they own a flaming house!' Alice exclaimed, a loud enough outburst that Mavis poked her head round the kitchen door.

'Sorry, Mavis,' Norman said, offering his best apologetic father expression. He turned to face Alice and said, 'We did tell you, you just took it the wrong way.'

'Because we spend too much time in this family being sarcastic. Who in their right mind gives someone a house?'

'Well, your Aunty Magdalena for one. She thought it would be a nice gesture'

'She signed it over to you to avoid paying duties should she die.'

'And now she's dead.' Alice leaned forward, placed her elbows on the table and clutched at her hair. She shook her head, groaning. Over the course of two days, she'd lost her job, been smeared in the newspaper and gained a house.

'We thought she'd let you move in when she emigrated, but she said it was too risky.'

'How was it risky? She lives in Partridge Mews. It's hardly the ganglands.'

'It'll be because Roger and his lot were around putting the frighteners on.'

'I'm guessing Duke is still going in to check on things?'

Norman nodded. 'He hasn't run into much trouble. Roger has tried to force his way in before now, but he didn't get far.'

'At least he's conscientious,' said Primrose.

'He's an idiot, Mum. Would you try breaking and entering when there's a former detective next door?' Arthur might be past his prime, but Alice guaranteed he still knew a thing or two about apprehending criminals.

'I'd like to think I'd never resort to a life of crime.'

'Says the woman drinking green tea.'

'Be fair, Alice, that's not a crime. It's just plain dozy.' Mavis had arrived with their food: two all day breakfasts, and a Greek salad for Primrose. It was one of the healthier suggestions on Mavis's menu; stolen from Delia Smith when the local Bulge Busters complained about the lack of sensible food choices for those mindful of their waist measurements.

'Thanks Mavis, I've always appreciated your honesty. It's one of the reasons I still come here after all these years. To be insulted.'

'I'm glad to hear it. I don't know how I'd go on if I found out you'd gone elsewhere.' Mavis flashed a bawdy grin and headed back to the kitchen.

Norman and Alice handed the salt and pepper to one another. 'I suppose we should talk about what you want to do, Alice.'

'What do you mean?'

'Well you're twenty-five now, and most of your friends don't live with their parents anymore.'

'Are you kicking me out?' Alice asked, a piece of fried egg dangling precariously on her fork.

'No, nothing like that. It's just considering you don't have a job, it might be best to put that energy into doing the place up.'

'I was in social care, not architecture.'

'It'll be a learning curve.'

'And you're sure you're not in the middle of a mid-life crisis?'

'I could be, but I've also got a bit of a selfish reason.'

'What's that?'

'Duke might have warned Roger off before, but after the way you decked him today, I wouldn't be surprised if he forced his way in and took everything, down to the soft furnishings.'

Alice mulled this over as she dipped her sausage in her egg yolk. 'We'll go this afternoon,' she said.

Chapter Four

Aunty Magdalena lived in Partridge Mews, the next town over. At least, she had before the business in Madeira and her subsequent death. She bought her millstone cottage on Falstaff Close in the 1960s, a time when houses were cheap. Her second husband had just left her after his funny business behind the cricket pavilion came to light. Divorce suited Aunty Magdalena, and she would go on to break the hearts of many.

Though Alice didn't care much for the town, she'd always found a home away from home at Aunty Magdalena's. She couldn't imagine entering without the presence of one of her greatest female role models.

She hadn't been to the cottage for over a year. She knew that the place was being looked after, and she'd convinced herself that things would sour between Aunty Magdalena and her new husband and she'd come back, reopen her homeopathy clinic and have an abundance of cake in the pantry.

'She taught me how to bake,' Alice said from the back seat of her father's Peugeot. Hedgerows surrounded them on all sides as they travelled the short route down an old country lane towards Partridge Mews. The weather remained pleasant; sunlight cast dappled shadows over them.

It was the kind of spring weather that inspires nostalgia. Alice recalled days spent in the kitchen, getting the hang of recipes, sharing cakes with her friends, and dreaming of competing on Ready Steady Cook.

Soon enough, Norman pulled up outside the cottage.

It looked no different. There was no visible sign that the cottage had lost its owner.

'Do we even have keys?' Alice asked. She felt anxiety kneading at her forehead, and a gurgling in her stomach that she was certain didn't stem from Mavis's food.

'Of course, we have the keys, love. I never take them out of my handbag.'

Alice nodded, swallowing hard. She locked eyes with Norman in his rear-view mirror.

His gaze tinged with concern, and he cocked his head to the side. 'What's wrong, Al?'

Tears stung her eyes like hot needles. Alice shook her head. 'I don't think I can go in there.'

Norman and Primrose were soon at her sides, squeezing her into the middle of the back seat. Alice allowed an aria of sobs to rise from her chest. She buried her face in her father's shirt, unable to stem the tears. 'Why couldn't she just sell the place? She had to be so ruddy complicated.'

'It's been a bit intense, these last couple of days, Al. It's no surprise you're overwrought.'

'Overwrought? A dead aunty, a lost job, and a new house. They weren't wrong when they said bad things came in threes.' Alice pressed at her eyes as though her palms were Kleenex.

'Maybe your father and I got a bit carried away. We should've waited a few days, allowed you to properly acclimatise to the situation.'

'I can't acclimatise to the situation, Mum.' Alice turned on Primrose, her face a funny shade of luncheon meat.

'Now–'

'No, Dad. Aunty Magdalena is dead. There were no goodbyes, no funeral, nothing.'

'We talked about that.'

'I know. I *know*. I understand, but I miss her. I miss her more than I thought possible.' Her chest ached from the effort of crying, as though some goblin were inside her, all set to dismantle her ribcage. She felt empty, hollow, her throat scraped empty.

Primrose rummaged through her handbag until she came across a tissue. She handed it over. 'It's a bit scrunched, but it'll do the job.'

As Alice dabbed at her face, Norman spoke. He said, 'I know this will sound like I'm trying to diminish your grief, but I'm not. We all miss Aunty Magdalena. She was my favourite of your grandad's siblings, and from the moment you were conceived, she needed to play a major role in your upbringing.

'Maybe I shouldn't have done. Maybe I should've left you with your Mum's friends more. At least then you wouldn't be feeling like this.'

Norman stroked tear-soaked hair away from Alice's eyes.

She sniffed. 'I still have to experience grief, Dad. No matter who you do or don't introduce me to.'

'Alice is right, love.' Primrose took to stroking Alice's hands as though they were degloved kittens. 'I don't mean to be pushy. I understand not wanting to go inside, believe me, but I don't want this house to become a place of sadness for you.'

'How can it be anything else?'

'That's just maudlin, and we certainly didn't raise you that way.'

'A minute ago, you were telling me it was all right if I didn't want to go inside.'

'And it is, but this is Aunty Magdalena's cottage.' Primrose put on her consoling face, ever the cartoon cat after tuna.

Alice turned to her father. 'And what do you think?' she asked.

'Come off it, Al, you've never needed my opinion to make a decision before.'

'Well I'm asking for it now.'

Norman smiled that knowing smile so common with fathers and said, 'I think your Mum is right. We don't *have* to go inside now, but I think we should.'

Alice shrank down in the seat and balled up the tissue in her hands. She craved a cocoon, to go home, to get into bed and to say no to the world for a few days. Yet that would feel too much like failing, like she was treating Aunty Magdalena's death in the same way she treated breaking up with her last boyfriend, hidden for days, too ashamed to admit she'd failed at love. She recalled how Aunty Magdalena had turned up in her bedroom with a picnic and called her foolish. No, she deserved to be remembered properly and Alice was the only appropriate candidate.

She swallowed hard; her throat felt like she'd swallowed a jellyfish. She clenched her fists, alabaster fingers against red palms, and said, 'Let's go inside.'

She ignored her parents as they smiled to one

another.

They should have stayed outside.

Aunty Magdalena might have employed a caretaker to look after the place, but he'd clearly not been doing his job. The exterior lied to them, with its well-tended garden. The herbaceous border was spectacular; asters, hollyhocks and poppies vied for attention, bright splashes of colour amongst masses of greenery. Once, the cottage's walls had been weighed down by ivy, looking as though the building were in chains, as though nature fought back and held the house to ransom. Now, the ivy had been cleared. Despite years of claims that it added character to the place, the lack of ivy eliminated the dilapidated air that had previously surrounded the cottage.

The birds didn't help, either. Chaffinches chirped an early afternoon ditty that lent itself well to the spring day with its agreeable weather, blue skies and white clouds, fluffy enough to inspire calm. The outside of the house was an estate agent's dream.

It was enough to lull Alice into a false sense of security, certain that Marmaduke Featherstone had been hard at work, keeping the place tidy.

The three of them wandered down the path, admiring Duke's handiwork. Primrose commented on the fresh air and the close proximity to the woods. Alice just had to cross the stream in the back garden, and she'd be amongst the trees. In the past, Aunty Magdalena would forage in the woods for her homeopathy business, like an old boar after truffles.

Whilst Aunty Magdalena had allowed them to replace her windows with double glazing, she outright refused to modernise her front door. It looked more suited to a stable, a shed or an outside privy than a cottage. It was white, with large black bolts all down its front. The hinges encroached upon a great deal of the door, as though reminding all visitors it wasn't a wall or some forgotten portcullis.

The door wasn't the problem.

It was when Norman opened the door that they realised something was awry.

An indescribable stench attacked their nostrils, somewhere between stale body odour and rotten pork. The smell brought to mind images of school gyms on stifling summer days, and butchers' shops with no refrigeration.

The three of them looked at each other with grimaces on their faces, not unlike three nauseous gargoyles.

'I don't think Febreze will fix this,' Alice said.

They stepped into the hall. Family photographs lined the walls, on a path towards the kitchen.

They turned left and entered the living room.

It was a mess.

Alice's eyes widened so much that she could've been a snail. Cobwebs clung to the drawn curtains. The stench was worse here, and it was little wonder for the place was fit to bursting with bin bags that were filled, stretched tight and leaking. Every now and then, there'd be a banana skin.

Alice heard the snoring before she saw the man. It was a guttural growling, snarling sound, as though his mouth was an exhaust and his lungs a starter motor.

She followed the sound to see the hulking shadow on the sofa. The red Arighi Bianchi sofa. The one that had cost a tenth of Aunty Magdalena's fourth divorce settlement. The same sofa that now housed a few takeaway trays, old newspapers, empty cider bottles, and one very unkempt older man.

Alice stormed over to the curtains and flung them open, bathing the room in sunlight. Only this sunlight didn't wash away evil, it emphasised it. Every bin bag seemed greasier, and the light highlighted the fact that they were caked in dust.

The light also served to awaken the slumbering man. He groaned and rubbed his eyes. A leonine figure, his greying mane rose from his scalp like an unruly tumbleweed. He yawned, something like a yowl, and pulled his stained t-shirt down over his midriff.

'Rise and shine, Marmaduke,' Alice said. 'You've got some explaining to do.'

Marmaduke blinked a few times and stared blearily at Alice, his blue eyes dewy with sleep. 'Whaddayawan?' he said, his words a nonsensical jumble.

Alice found herself reminded of the Beast from the Disney film. He was a great lumbering cat of a man.

The sight of him made Alice's blood boil. She swept her hair away from her face and said, more as a yell than anything, 'I want to know what the heck you think you're doing!'

Marmaduke was clearly too tired to understand what she was talking about. He was as groggy as an inebriated monk after mass as he said, 'I'm looking after this cottage for a friend of mine.'

'It's us, Duke,' Norman said.

'You might want to put your glasses on, love.'

'Yes, put your glasses on so you can see what a mess you've made.'

'Alice -'

'We put our trust in this, this … oaf, and he's turned the cottage into a pig sty.' Alice rounded on

Marmaduke. He froze in search of his spectacles and met Alice's gaze once again. 'Well,' she said, 'aren't you even going to try to explain yourself?'

Marmaduke located his glasses in a takeaway tray, coated in a viscous brown liquid. It was something like treacle, only fouler, and liable to strip the paintwork off a Ford Anglia. He looked at them all despondently as the sauce dripped into the container.

Alice continued to glower at him, her arms folded. Norman watched, aghast. He'd never been able to cope with foreign liquids; he even struggled with tiramisu. Only Primrose took pity on Marmaduke. She crossed the room and took the container from his hands before she'd finished uttering, 'Oh, give them here, love.'

'Mum!'

'He has cataracts, Alice.'

'Does that mean he doesn't know his way to the bin?'

'It might look bad now, Alice, but it's easily remedied,' Marmaduke said.

'Yes, we knock you on the head and say you died in your own filth.'

Marmaduke grinned. He sank back against the sofa, crinkling as he went. 'That's the spirit. I always knew we'd get on.'

Alice was flabbergasted.

Primrose returned from the kitchen with Marmaduke's glasses, allowing Alice time to gather her thoughts. 'Now, love,' she said, 'why don't you tell us just what all this mess is about?'

'I'm on surveillance,' he said. He put his glasses on to punctuate his sentence, his eyes magnified by his thick lenses, looking somewhat like the offspring of a hawk and a milk bottle.

'That's all well and good, but what exactly are you surveilling?' Primrose patted his arm. Alice hoped her mother was trying to kill him with kindness.

Marmaduke crumpled. He folded his arms like a petulant schoolboy and, huffing, said, 'I'm afraid I can't tell you that, Primrose. Confidential information, that is.'

'Listen here, you ancient toe-rag,' Alice said. 'I don't care about who or what you're supposedly surveilling. You could be the biggest Peeping Tom in all of Partridge Mews for all I care. I simply want to know why you've treated my aunty's house like it's some godawful dumping ground.'

Norman, ever the diplomat, said, 'I'll put the kettle on,' and scarpered into the kitchen.

Marmaduke pressed his tongue against his teeth as though testing their integrity. He sat a bit straighter in his seat and, with no hint of sarcasm, said, 'It's not that bad, for a doss house.'

He anticipated the first takeaway tray and managed to dodge it, only for Alice to hit him right between the eyes with her next projectile.

Alice tore through the bags like a badger through a dustbin, unable to find anything firm or heavy enough to knock some sense into Marmaduke Featherstone.

'How dare you?' she exclaimed. 'We ask you to be caretaker of the cottage in good faith, and you have the audacity to sit there and take the Mick.'

Alice caught hold of something beneath one of the bin bags and pulled it free. She'd only just raised it over her head when her mother said, 'Alice, stop.'

Primrose had watched Alice with eyes as wide as a cartoon rabbit, not knowing how to put a stop to the rampage. 'Do you honestly believe Aunty Magdalena would want that kind of behaviour in her house?'

'I thought we'd agreed it was my house now.' Alice sneered, at the point of anger when scoring cheap shots is more important than sense.

'You know what I mean.' Primrose stepped cautiously towards Alice. 'I don't condone what Duke has done, but even if you don't think about your aunty, think about how this will look.'

Alice's shoulders drooped. 'What do you mean?'

'Throw anything else and folk will think you've got something against older people.'

Her cheeks were flushed. 'You're right.'

'Besides, look what you were about to throw.'

It was a photograph of Alice and Aunty Magdalena from her seventieth birthday celebrations. The oak frame suddenly felt as heavy as an articulated truck.

Alice's chest fluttered once again. She breathed deeply before setting the picture back down. 'You're lucky my mother's here, Duke.'

Duke rubbed the sore spot on his head. 'Lucky you have a reputation for killing old folk, you mean?'

'Mrs Cameron was a menace! Besides, how can the death of one old woman give me a reputation?'

'You know this town, Alice. From now on, this is how you'll be remembered.'

'Marmaduke, give it a rest, will you?' Norman said, stepping over the bin bags with a tray of tea and biscuits.

'Did you honestly wait until I'd finished throwing things before saying something?'

'I didn't want to get caught in the crossfire.'

'You were hiding behind the fridge door.'

'I was looking for the milk.'

'We could see you.'

'If I'd brought the tea in whilst you were throwing all and sundry then you'd have hit me. I'd have been knocked down, spilling tea all over Marmaduke. They'd arrest you for assault and have me as an accomplice.' Norman crunched a chocolate bourbon.

'You do have an imagination, don't you, love?' Primrose placed a consoling hand on her husband's arm. 'Now that you've all calmed down a bit, perhaps Duke wouldn't mind telling us why the house is in such a state of disarray.' She fixed him with her most inquisitive glare, the motherly one used to extract all sorts of information.

Marmaduke furrowed his brow, his face screwed up in a grimace so that he looked like an old potato, with his tanned skin, his wrinkles, and his caterpillar eyebrows that resembled a line of mould. He looked as shifty as a milkman as he said to them, 'It's as I told you, Primrose. I'm on surveillance.'

'Yes, I think we understood that. But who, or what are you surveilling? And why use this house?'

'Why do you need to know?'

Alice clenched her mug of tea so hard that her fingers looked like Spam. 'We need to know because this is my house you've turned into your own personal tip.'

'You ask someone to look after your house, you've got to expect a bit of mess.'

'Pie crumbs on the draining board, but not a landfill site in the living room.' She kicked a bag for emphasis, only for it to squelch, topple, and spill its contents atop the rest of the rubbish.

Alice glowered.

This led to Marmaduke shrinking back in his chair, looking ever more like a tortoise in a t-shirt. He peeked at her before clamping his eyes shut.

'You can shut your eyes as tight as you like, Marmaduke, but we can still see you. You're no toddler, you know?'

Alice grew tired with her mother's kindness towards the man. She held her tongue, however, choosing a united front this time around.

After a few more minutes of silence, broken only by tea slurping and biscuit crunching, Marmaduke chose to open his eyes. He looked positively chastised as he said, 'It's supposed to be all hush-hush really, but I suppose it won't do any harm to tell you, you more or less being outsiders.'

'We only live in Wren's Lea.'

'Primrose is a member of your WI.'

'Alice was basically raised here.'

'Do you want to know who's under surveillance or not?' The Valentines went quiet, allowing Marmaduke to speak, 'Right, well. Since he seems to have gone completely off the deep end, and he's a friend of mine, I've been keeping an eye on Arthur Sterling.'

'What do you mean, "He's gone off the deep end?"' Alice asked.

He helped himself to a biscuit. 'It's like this, you see. A couple of years back – well your parents will remember this – the heir of Greenfields was murdered.'

'A couple of years,' Norman said, agog, 'Marmaduke, that's got to be fifty years ago.'

'Definitely before your time, love,' Primrose said to him.

'You can't have been that old yourself, Prim.'

She shrugged. 'I must've been about three. All I remember is being rushed off home before I got a go on the Tombola.'

'How does all this relate to Mr Sterling?' Alice asked.

'He was a constable at the time. A regular village bobby. There'd been some threats made and Arthur was tasked with establishing a police presence at the Greenfields Fete.'

'Yet he failed to save the man he was supposed to protect.'

Marmaduke nodded. 'The murderer hit Arthur first – clobbered the both of them over the head. It just happens that Arthur survived and Christopher Partridge met his maker.'

'And I'm guessing the murderer wasn't found?'

'There was no evidence, see? No murder weapon – and Arthur didn't see his attacker.'

'And now he's trying to figure out whodunit?' Primrose said. She'd reached the end of her biscuits, left with nothing more than a broken custard cream.

'It all started after his Ethel died. Any man would grieve, but Arthur threw himself into investigating this old case. He's been going to the library religiously, looking at old newspapers, scouring the internet, and when that turned up nothing he began pestering the locals.'

'I suppose that's when you took it upon yourself to move in here?' Alice said. She rocked her legs back and forth, rustling the bin bags. Somewhere beneath them all was a chair, a well-cushioned, cosy chair that would now, undoubtedly, stink of sweaty rubber.

'I had to so I could make sure.'

'Make sure of what?'

'Arthur's burned a lot of bridges. I wouldn't be surprised if someone turned up here planning to do him a mischief.'

Alice bobbed her head once. 'Right. Now tell us just

why you could only observe Arthur from under a mountain of filth.'

They all looked at him expectantly.

'I wanted folk to think the place was abandoned – that no one was looking in on the place.'

'Despite that being completely senseless, it's all got to go.' Alice bristled with a glint in her eyes. 'No more surveillance. I'm moving in.'

Chapter Five

Marmaduke protested, of course, but two weeks later he allowed Alice to take ownership of the cottage. At least she was able to enter and begin the clean-up operation, because after Marmaduke cited everything from sciatica to age to hoarding, Alice realised it would be easier to do it herself.

Hence she was in a hardware store at eight-thirty in the morning in search of a mop bucket. The place reeked of white spirits and wood shavings, a veritable shrine to Sunday afternoons cleaning out the garage.

She hadn't been in there long when two older men entered, clearly in the midst of a discussion. One of them, she didn't know. He had greying hair and wore overalls that had yet to be dirtied. The other, she recognised straight away, simply by the shock of white hair. Mr Sterling. Not surprising, since this was his brother's shop.

'No, Ronnie, we can't. Suppose someone should find out?'

'But it wasn't me.'

'You did time, remember? It was your gun.'

'How many times? The gun was stolen.'

'And the money?' Mr Sterling's eyes were as inquisitive as a teacher reprimanding a student over the misuse of a yo-yo.

This also coincided with the two men catching sight of Alice's reflection in the security mirror above the till. They didn't know she was there until she walked into the metal mop buckets, betrayed by her own curiosity in their conversation.

The men hushed up immediately. Mr Sterling brushed down his shirt before walking to the top of Alice's aisle. 'Good morning,' he said, the grin on his face doing nothing to diminish the red of his cheeks.

Alice willed her shoulders to relax. 'Morning' she mumbled back with a silent familiarity.

'Sorry you heard us going at it.'

'It's fine. Really. Not what you expect when you go out to buy a mop bucket, but it's fine.'

'We've been friends for so long that when we disagree…well, you know what it's like.'

Alice picked up a mop bucket. 'Are you able to serve me?'

Mr Sterling visibly relaxed. 'But of course.'

'Then I can leave you to get on with your chat.'

The two men chuckled falsely as Mr Sterling rang the bucket through the till.

Alice thanked him and left. The uneasiness didn't dissipate as she walked away. She clenched the mop bucket with a grip the Hulk would have been proud of. Mr Sterling had mentioned a gun and a robbery, and he and his friend were hiding something, that was easy enough to grasp. Granted, Alice knew it was none of her business, but there wasn't much else to think about besides tidying up. Perhaps Mr Sterling was getting closer to finding his killer. Alice hoped so. He was grieving – if he found Christopher Partridge's assailant, he might start to process the loss of his wife.

Alice returned to the cottage.

The bin liners were still there.

As was a little old man. He sat on the sofa looking as unobtrusive as a Munchkin on a rugby pitch.

'Who are you?' she asked.

'Well, you see, I'd rather not say if you don't mind. I'd prefer to keep it confidential, if you like.'

Alice set the mop bucket down gently, aware she could throw it at any given opportunity. She breathed deeply, an attempt to calm down that did nothing and left her looking like an asthmatic near an aerosol. Alice chose the illusion of calm instead, wondered just what her mother would do and said, 'I'm sorry, but I need to know your name before we continue this conversation.'

The man remained wary. He was so scrawny that his red fleece looked fit to swallow him. If Alice was being honest, the man's head looked like a turnip, squat and wrinkled, with tufts of yellowy-white hair sticking up all over the place. This turnip-headed man would be great as the professor in an am-dram production of *Back to the Future*.

Alice decided to try a different tack. She was supposedly a trained social worker, so she should know how to talk to people. 'If you don't want to tell me your name,' she said, in the tone she usually reserved for toddlers, 'why don't you tell me why you're here?'

He continued to stare at his lap. 'My name's Ernie,' he said, on some sort of two-minute delay.

Alice headed towards the kitchen. 'I'll make a brew, Ernie. Maybe you can have a think about what you want to say.'

'It's more something I'd have to show you.'

Alice got the mugs out of the cupboard, saying, 'If you think that would be best.'

When Alice awoke that morning, she had expected to have a simple day, tidying and going to the tip. She hadn't expected to see an OAP's unmentionables. But when she turned back to talk to Ernie, he had his trousers around his ankles, his private parts definitely not private.

'What are you doing?' Alice exclaimed. She screwed her eyes shut tight and spun back around.

Ernie murmured apologetically. 'He said as you'd be able to help me. He said as you were a homeopath.'

'Who did?'

'That one who used to work for the police.'

'Mr Sterling?' Alice faced him again.

Ernie had pulled his trousers up, thankfully. He shrugged. 'I don't know, could be.'

'My aunty was the homeopath.'

'Is she here?'

'Only in spirit.'

'Oh.'

'Yes, oh. Anyway, that still doesn't explain why you think it's all right to drop your undercrackers at the merest encouragement.'

'I thought you were a homeopath, I couldn't exactly take it to my doctor. It's a delicate subject.'

'It's the first time I've heard it called that,' Alice said, grinning.

'Are you sure you can't help me? Only I've got a date with Janice Dooley and I can't see her like this, can I?'

'All right, Ernie. I'm not a trained homeopath, nor am I a qualified expert on male genitalia. How do you expect me to help?'

Ernie sighed. 'I suppose I hoped you might – being of the female persuasion yourself – I hoped you might have a solution to my problem.'

'I don't know what the problem is. I didn't exactly get an in-depth appraisal.'

'I see.' Ernie reached for his waistband.

Alice grabbed his wrists before he had a chance to expose himself yet again. She cursed whoever thought elasticated waists were a good thing to give to men. Men spent their lives itching to share their bits with the world.

She pinned Ernie's arms against his sides and said, 'How about you just tell me what the problem is?'

'I've got myself in a bit of an embarrassing predicament.'

Alice willed him to go on, relaxing her grip a bit, but not enough for him to be able to make any untoward advances at his tracksuit bottoms.

'You see, I've been chatting with this woman.'

'Janice?'

'No.'

'Who?'

'It's not important. We met at the Hare and Horse. Either way, we get chatting and end up back at hers.'

Alice had to hand it to Ernie. He may have been elderly and looked like something the greengrocer would throw in the compost, but to have amorous intentions at his age meant there was hope for humanity yet. 'So what happened?'

'We're on her sofa, getting down to business, when she stops me and asks if I've trimmed. I'll admit, I looked at her a bit gone out. I didn't know what she were on about. Then she springs it on me, she does, she says as she can't even think about touching a man who isn't completely clean-shaven down there.'

Alice couldn't believe what she heard. She looked at Ernie, mouth open, catching flies, before she said, 'What did you do?'

'I told her that I'm a bloke and it's an untamed topiary. She sent me off into the bathroom with a razor and the promise we could do whatever I wanted when I returned.'

'I'm guessing you now have an itchy rash.'

Ernie nodded, silent once more.

'Just shove some natural yoghurt on it. It'll calm down soon enough.'

Ernie blinked a few times, eyelashes flapping like butterflies on a desk fan. 'Is that it?'

'Yup.'

Ernie nodded. 'And I'm not supposed to eat it?'

'Nobody eats natural yoghurt, Ernie. It was invented for sado-masochists and Weight Watchers.'

'You're sure it'll work?'

Alice shrugged. 'No idea, but I'm not a homeopath. You're lucky I don't charge you.'

'We're done?'

'We're done,' Alice affirmed. 'But first, could you tell me how you got in?'

'Through the door.'

'I guessed that. You're not likely to climb through the window.'

'The door was unlocked,' he said, anticipating Alice's question before she could ask it.

'You've got to be joking.' Alice ran her hands over her face and through her hair, holding the strands above her head with little idea what to do next. She let the hair fall. 'I'm going to kill Marmaduke.'

'That's the man!' Ernie said, his eyes as wide as a

pleased pup that's just done his business outside for the first time.

'Sorry?'

'The man who sent me here. It wasn't Mr Sterling. It was Marmaduke.'

Alice nodded, seething. Her jaw looked tight enough to crack Brazil nuts as she said, 'I'm going to have to ask you to leave, Ernie. I've got some business to attend to.'

Ernie looked at her, oblivious. Slowly, realisation dawned on him and he nodded with a grin on his face, as gormless as a grapefruit. 'I best be going then.'

Alice walked him to the front door, wishing she'd stayed downwind. Ernie stank, a mixture of talcum powder and over-boiled cabbage. Before he left, however, it transpired he had more to say. 'I don't want anyone to get into trouble over me being here. See, the locks on these old cottages have always been a bit hit and miss.'

'Thanks for telling me, Ernie.' She urged him towards the door.

'I mean, usually I'd wait outside, but with this being a business, I wondered if maybe that were the way of things.'

'Yes, well, like I said, I do need to be getting on. Why don't you get down to the supermarket now, before your big date?'

Ernie shrugged. 'She's not really one for ceremony, is Janice. Anyway, I were just wondering – what are all those bags doing in your living room? Only, I don't think the bin men will be too happy.'

Alice tensed her hands and stared at the air just above Ernie's left ear. 'It's for the charity shop. Now kindly push off. We wouldn't want that rash to get infected, would we? Could be some nasty consequences.' She stepped forward, forcing Ernie out of the door, which she promptly slammed behind her.

She watched him scurry down the path, his head low, like a self-conscious mole.

Once Alice was certain he'd disappeared, she strode out. Her footsteps crunched against the stones. She moved with such anger that should so much as a millimetre of gravel slip into her shoes, she'd tear up the path and replace it with a moat.

Marmaduke Featherstone was fast becoming a thorn in her side. Not only had he made Aunty Magdalena's cottage look as though it belonged on an episode of Hoarders, but also he'd chosen to make the move as difficult as he possibly could.

She stormed up the road and froze, stopped stock still. She wasn't sure why it caught her eye, but she looked up anyhow.

Mr Sterling's door was open. Ajar, even. As though someone wanted to close the door but couldn't quite figure it out.

Thoughts of his recent arguments ran through Alice's mind. She edged towards his gate, uneasiness causing the hairs on the back of her neck to twitch. Alice couldn't understand the sense of something not quite being right. It made no sense how alert her mind became, how each crunch of her sole against gravel sounded like a landmine, how each flower petal wanted to be a gun, or a gloved hand, some masked assailant waiting in the shadows.

The front door creaked as she pushed it open. Her palms were as sweaty as they'd been on GCSE results day.

The living room curtains were drawn, leaving the

place in darkness, a blue hue cast over everything.

'Mr Sterling?' Alice called, voice quaking.

She caught sight of his hair first, a thatch of white straw rising from the armchair.

'Mr Sterling?'

Alice held her breath and listened intently. The room remained silent. She prayed for the sound of his heavy breathing, the guttural snoring of an old man.

Nothing.

Perhaps he was a light sleeper.

No, he wasn't. There was too much blood.

Alice noticed the thick clods of blood staining the mantelpiece, first. It coated the picture frames and the table beside him, just missing the trilby on the floor. She held back her screaming and made her way over to stand in front of him. His mouth hung open, blue eyes void and staring at nothing in particular.

Arthur Sterling was dead.

Chapter Six

Alice rang the first person to pop into her head.

'Hello,' he answered promptly, his gruff words masking a clog of phlegm held in the back of his throat.

Alice inhaled. Although she'd been a social worker for a short amount of time, she'd had some training – how to deal with difficult situations – but there'd been nothing about finding an elderly gentleman with his head caved in.

'He's dead, Duke. Mr Sterling's been killed.'

Marmaduke didn't answer immediately. His breathing slowed down, still the rattle of an old man. Eventually, he spoke, his words measured, saying, 'All right, Alice. What I want you to do is to get photographs. Take as many as you can – of Arthur, the room, anything you think important.'

Alice nodded, her entire body trembling as though she was a ball of static electricity. She switched her phone to speaker and had turned on the camera by the time that sense took over. 'Won't the police do this themselves? Why do I need to take photographs?' Still, she followed his instructions, beginning with a panoramic shot of the room.

'These aren't for the police.'

Alice froze, her finger over the button. 'Please don't tell me these are for your own personal collection. If you have some weird fetish, I don't want any part in fulfilling your desires.'

'Just take the photos. I'm on my way over – I'll ring the police.'

The line went dead.

She knew she shouldn't be entertaining Marmaduke's whims. Yet hadn't he thought something like this would happen to Mr Sterling? And Alice had forced him from her home, couldn't see past her own rage towards him, and now a man sat dead; murdered in his own armchair.

Once she'd taken what she deemed was an adequate number of photos, she went outside to wait for Marmaduke. There was nothing she could do for Mr Sterling now.

The blue sky was the wrong colour. It ought to be bleaker, all greys and thunderous, more in keeping with the events of the morning.

It rained the day that Aunty Magdalena died. At least, it rained the day Alice learned about it. Nobody bothered to let her know until she'd been cremated, and her husband acquitted of foul play. Alice wondered if that was why no one had told her – because they knew that at the first suggestion someone had done away with her aunty, she'd be on the first plane to Madeira, all set to perform her own brand of capital punishment.

She picked at her cuticles, each small pin drop of red doing nothing to erase the lozenge of grief in her throat.

Marmaduke arrived within the next quarter of an hour. He no longer looked like something a dustbin would throw up. Gone were the jogging bottoms and Bullseye t-shirt. Marmaduke wore a pair of tartan trousers and a freshly ironed, Daz-white shirt. His shoes were polished to within an inch of their lives. And over it all, he wore a brown duffel overcoat.

'You look like an advert for a Scottish funeral company,' Alice said. 'Did you misplace your bagpipes?'

'In my trousers, if you fancy a blow.' His eyes glinted, ever the rogue.

'I'm going to pretend you didn't say that.'

'Probably for the best. Did you get the photos?'

'I still don't understand why we need them.'

'I told you.'

'You didn't.'

He eyed her for a moment, then shrugged it off. 'They'll be useful in our investigation.'

'What do you mean? You're not a policeman anymore.'

'I know.'

'You've no DNA testing, no CSI, no team.' Alice stood staring at him, eyes agog, praying her words would sink in.

'I believe I'm what they call a freelancer.'

'I believe it's illegal.

He chuckled, sounding something like a pompous lion. 'You can't worry about things like that. I was in the force for nearly fifty years, and I'm an OAP.'

'You can still get arrested if you're an OAP.'

'Only if you get caught.'

Alice rolled her eyes and remained quiet, certain she'd been a complete monster in a previous life to be plagued by so many overbearing elders. She blamed Aunty Magdalena. If she hadn't been socialised so much as a child, then Alice could well be on her way to being a reject from Jeremy Kyle. It wasn't the life she wanted. She sometimes grew tired of the quality within her that said she must entertain the whims of all and sundry, even if that meant taking corpse photos for a would-be private detective.

A few minutes later, the sound of sirens cut through the air like a steak knife through silk. The familiar blues and reds flashed. Their butterfly after-image pressed against the back of Alice's eyelids.

The officers vacated their cars.

Alice's mouth fell open. 'I can't be here,' she said, as the officers approached. Yet it was only one who caused her intestines to rise up and strangle her vocal cords, eliciting the sweat on her mid-riff, the rising heat of her cheeks.

Her mind flew back years. Alice was sixteen again, sneaking out of the cinema to go and meet a muscular farmhand in the car park.

Only this wasn't that man.

This was the man she'd left behind with the excuse that she wanted her own popcorn. This was …

'Jeremy?'

He blinked at her a few times, doing a rather good job of pretending he couldn't place her face, unless of course he actually couldn't. His silence allowed Alice the chance to take in his appearance.

He looked good – not that one can look fashionable in pastel blue shirt and plain black trousers – but everything was fitted, emphasising that here was a man who clearly worked out.

And he was a policeman. A policeman who couldn't remember her name.

Alice's stomach gurgled. She pressed a hand against her abdomen, her face the dictionary definition of embarrassed, all ruddy cheeks and shifty gaze.

She was having none of it. 'I haven't changed that much in nine years, Jeremy.'

He cocked his head to the side, his eyes inquisitive. 'I reckoned you had to be someone from school. I haven't heard that name in years.'

'You don't remember me?'

He shrugged. 'Should I?'

'It's me. Alice. Alice Valentine. I stood you up at the cinema in favour of Dan Brady.'

'Not really jogging my memory.' He looked from Alice to Marmaduke. 'I suppose one of you reported the murder.'

Marmaduke made to speak, but Alice said, 'You had a huge crush on me. Remember? You sent me that long, long message on MSN?'

Jeremy remembered. A wave of nostalgia flooded his body, his shoulders back, an intake of breath deep enough to keep him going for six months. He scratched the back of his hair – blonde, immaculate, impeccably-styled – and said, 'The thing is, Alice–'

She didn't hear what the thing was. A complete daddy-long-legs of a man stormed up the road towards them, running fast enough to blow his white wisps of hair back across his scalp. His grey anorak billowed into wings behind him so as he looked like an albino bat, or a train spotter who'd missed the 9:20 to Manchester.

'Clive, what're you doing here?' Marmaduke stopped the man in his tracks.

Jeremy stared with concern at Clive, at the heavy breathing, and the sweat streaming down his mottled forehead as though his body was trying to expunge itself of all fluid. 'You don't need to be here, sir.'

'He's my friend,' Clive said, heaving gasps.

'That may be so, but it isn't your job.'

'And it isn't your place to tell me my job, is it?' Clive glowered at Jeremy. He hissed through his teeth, a corpse grin as he strove to let the air into his lungs.

'The lad's right though, Clive. You shouldn't be here.'

'Then we say I'm not here on any official capacity, but I need to see my friend. I owe him that much.'

Alice watched the exchange, detached from the conversation. She watched Jeremy's fellow officers staring over, their own conversations interrupted by the arrival of this Clive, a man they all knew, who was clearly a colleague – of a fashion.

She chewed on her cuticles before saying, 'Maybe we should all just go inside.'

Clive's wild eyes were now on her. 'And you are?'

Alice couldn't help herself – she rolled her eyes. 'And here I was, thinking everyone in this town knew me.'

'Well?'

'I'm Alice. I'm the one who just found a man with his head caved in, so maybe you could stop looking at me like I just stole your ham sandwich.'

The air grew thick with tension.

Alice had her fists clenched.

Jeremy looked between the two of them, as though picking a side.

Marmaduke met Alice's gaze, his look a mixture of incredulity and pride.

And Clive.

Clive blinked a few times at Alice, looking somewhat like a child who's never been told off before. 'Duke phoned it in,' he said.

Alice nodded. 'He did. I found the body and rang

him. I had no idea who else to ring.'

'Maybe 999,' Jeremy said. 'Duke hasn't been in the force for years.'

'I'm sorry, Jeremy. I'd just found a corpse, I wasn't really thinking straight.'

'It's Jez. My name is Jez.' He practically growled at her.

'No need to be so tetchy. Shall we go inside?'

'We will, you're not,' Clive said.

'Why the heck not?'

'This is a crime scene, not a house party.'

'And what about Duke?'

'What about him?'

'Surely he's a civilian as well.' Alice couldn't help herself. She knew she should have kept her mouth shut, but there was nothing to be done now. She looked at the three of them and felt like an ant about to be trod on, as though she'd shrunk from the sheer force of their eyes. Of course, Duke would have special privileges. He'd been a detective, plain-clothes with the best of them, and Arthur Sterling had been a friend of his. He'd already expressed interest in the investigation. Alice hoped her words wouldn't cost him the opportunity.

'I've helped out on investigations before.'

'We know, Duke,' Jez said. 'But we don't even know that there'll be a need for an investigation.'

'He's been murdered.'

'Exactly. We know these cases are mostly paperwork. How many people would want to kill Arthur?'

'He was a detective, same as us. He'll have rubbed a lot of people the wrong way.'

Alice didn't care to mention the heated discussions

she'd been privy to. Although Mavis Thistlethwaite knew her way around a rolling pin, Alice doubted she'd close the café to knobble a pensioner in the next town over. She still felt like Marmaduke should be allowed to see the body, even if he had sent Ernie round to hers.

'Can't Duke go in, and if anyone brings it up you say he was helping in an advisory capacity?' Alice asked, feeling top of the class, keeping her smile cautious.

'You know I know my way around a crime scene.'

Both Jez and Clive didn't have immediate answers. They kept eyeing each other, communicating through subtle shoulder movements. Jez also seemed to enjoy swaying back and forth in his rather well-polished shoes.

'It's your call,' Jez said.

Clive conceded with a bow of his head. 'If anyone says anything, I'll square it with HR myself.'

Marmaduke shook his hand. 'That's really good of you, Clive.'

'I understand the need. It doesn't seem real.'

'I warned him. All along, I warned him.'

'We all did. He was making too many enemies.'

'One of whom clearly took it too far.'

After a few more minutes of conversation, they made their way up the drive.

Alice waited outside. She'd seen the body; she didn't particularly want to see it again. There was only so much corpse-viewing a person could do before they ended up contemplating the exact meaning of life, and Alice didn't need to entertain the idea of an existential crisis.

Twenty-five seemed the perfect age to question what she was doing with her life. Especially when the majority of her school-friends were married, getting married, with children or getting divorced. Granted, some of them were having children when they were still at school. Natalie Boothroyd missed her GCSEs because she was having Brooklyn. He'd be getting on for ten. No, Alice didn't feel that she'd missed out on anything by getting her degree and entering the workforce, but seeing people – her former peers – fulfil their societal obligations left her feeling disenchanted, as though she'd achieved nothing more in life than an encyclopaedic knowledge of *Legally Blonde*.

Perhaps avoiding the corpse hadn't done much to alleviate the deep-rooted feeling of wasting her life.

She leaned against the low, drystone wall at the edge of the garden. A few of the officers still paced outside, dawdling, scraping their shoes over the path.

Alice dug her fingernails into the cracks between the stones, scratching at cobweb wisps and wet moss. She stared at her shoelaces, feigning a great interest in the grass stain she found there.

Mr Sterling was dead, and all she felt was unbridled, thumb-twiddling boredom.

In fact, the most exciting moment came as Duke and the others left the cottage. They'd only made it a few steps down the path when a young woman called, 'Sir!' and came running from inside.

'What's the matter?' Clive asked, eyes alert.

'Your hat.' She handed him a tweed trilby.

He nodded in thanks before forcing it into the inner pocket of his coat.

They made their way back over to Alice, all looking paler than when they'd entered. They had the universal contemplative gait of men who were struggling between grief and maintaining a masculine façade.

Alice offered then a sympathetic smile. 'How are you

feeling?' she asked, though she didn't expect an answer.

'I've asked Detective Carson to take you home, Miss Valentine,' Clive said.

She stood up and rubbed her hands down the front of her jeans. 'Is this to do with the investigation?'

'You'll be asked some questions, yes.'

'Right then, Jezza,' Alice said. 'Come along. You'll have to excuse the mess.'

Chapter Seven

'You weren't joking,' Jez said, navigating his way around the bin bags to reach a spot of bare carpet.

'A necessary evil, apparently. Something about Duke making the place look disused for surveillance purposes.'

'Surveillance?'

'He knew there was something going on.'

Jez nodded. He scratched the back of his head with his pen.

'Would you like a brew?'

The mugs sat on the counter, waiting to be filled. Alice shook her head. Hers had been a day of elderly penis and corpse finding and she had no idea how to solve that problem. Although now she supposed she would just hand the matter over to the proper authorities and get back to some form of normality.

'Did you leave the back door open?' Jez asked. He wandered over and squatted beside a pile of dirt. Fresh dirt, dirt that had clearly been brought in on someone's shoes.

Alice crossed her arms, stifling the whimper that wished to air its opinion. Ernie came through the front door, she was sure of that much. 'Do you think it was the killer?'

Jez returned to her side. He spoke in what Alice thought of as his "policeman voice", all calm and soothing tones. 'I think it isn't right to speculate at this point. There's every chance it blew in from outside. These old doors aren't used to being locked.'

'Great, there's a killer loose in Partridge Mews, and he can waltz in here any time he likes.'

'Why don't you sit down? I'll make the drinks.'

Alice moved rubbish to make room for them both on the sofa. She tried not to think about Mr Sterling. Instead, she found memories of her schooldays swimming to the forefront of her mind. Specifically, memories of Jez.

He'd always seemed such a shy boy. He wore the sleeves of his blazer over his hands, always had headphones on and would hide behind the science department during breaks. And now he was a policeman, and he knew how to take care of himself. He was stylish. A revenge body if ever there was one. Alice just hoped it wasn't revenge against her for leaving him at the cinema.

'I was really surprised when you sent me that message, you know?' she said.

'What message?'

'On MSN, telling me you fancied me.'

'Oh,' he said, bringing the drinks over. 'That.'

'Yes, that. I stood you up and I want you know I'm sorry.'

Once again, he scratched the back of his head, eyes on some vague location. He looked shifty, like a person caught on a dirty website.

Alice cocked her head. 'What is it?' she said.

He gulped, put his Adam's apple to the test, and said, 'The thing is, Alice, well, MSN Messenger would refresh all the time, remember? You'd find the person you wanted to speak to and click their name, but every now and then someone would log in, and if you weren't careful you'd wind up messaging the wrong person.'

Alice's cheeks grew red, flushes of clotted beetroot. She tugged at her collar. 'You didn't mean to message me?'

He couldn't meet her eyes, shook his head. 'Afterwards, I tried to get in touch, but you were never online when I was.'

'Who did you really fancy, then?'

Jez took time with his answer, rubbing his hands, slurping his tea, becoming rather too interested in an antimacassar. 'Ben Weatherill.'

Alice allowed the name to settle. She blinked. Once. Twice. 'Oh, so you're…'

'Yeah.'

'Right.'

'I thought you realised at the cinema. Me and Ben were with each other when you arrived.'

Alice recalled the sticky floors and the hot popcorn air that felt as muggy as a rainforest. Now she thought about it, she remembered the two of them sharing a Coke and how she'd thought that they didn't have much cash between them. She didn't realise she was the third wheel.

'I met Dan Brady getting M&Ms. We flirted, and I thought I never wanted to see another *X-Men* film anyway,' Alice said.

'It was *The Da Vinci Code*.'

'What was?'

'The film we were seeing. It was *The Da Vinci Code*,

not *X-Men*.'

'Are you sure?'

'It was my first date with a boy. I'm pretty sure I'd remember.'

Alice groaned. 'Do you have to keep bringing it up?'

'You can't regret standing me up too much if you can't remember what film we were meant to be seeing.' He drank his coffee, looking smug.

Alice had no choice but to observe her reflection in her cup. 'So what's Ben up to now?'

'Married.'

'Yeah? Who's the lucky person?'

'Me.'

'What?' Alice's eyes widened so much that she looked like a startled goldfish. 'You're married!'

It was his turn to look shocked. 'I mean, it seemed like a natural progression.'

'Did you never want to play the field? Spread your little gay wings, sample dishes from exotic locations?'

Jez shrugged. 'We broke up the summer before uni. I was going travelling. When we finished, after other relationships, dalliances, all that stuff guys are supposed to do, we came home and started seeing each other again.'

She sank back into her sofa, praying it would swallow her whole. This served to emphasise the complete mess she'd made of things. It wasn't that she wanted marriage, just the success of something gone well, something that didn't serve as a reminder of her failures.

Alice pinched the bridge of her nose. 'I need a Pinot Grigio.'

'It's barely eleven o'clock in the morning.'

'You're a policeman, aren't you, Jeremy?'

'It's Jez.'

'I couldn't care less. So far this morning, an OAP has broken into my home and exposed himself, I've found the murdered body of a man I'd grown up around, and I just found out that you're married. Isn't it your responsibility as a twenty-first century homosexual to share that little tidbit of information on Facebook, Instagram, perhaps even LinkedIn? No, I'm having a terrible time, and I want a bleeding Pinot Grigio. Now tell me, in your professional opinion, would my actions be justified?'

'Should we just get on with the questions?'

Jez didn't stay much longer after Alice finished telling him about her morning. Not that there was much to tell. She chose to keep the photographs to herself. For some reason, she didn't think the police would be happy to hear she had images of their crime scene, especially images she'd collected on the instructions of Marmaduke Featherstone.

Once Jez left, she found herself back on the sofa, staring at the bin bags, contemplating. She had only gone out to purchase a mop bucket.

She checked the time.

Maybe Jez was right. Maybe it was too early for Pinot Grigio, but she couldn't help but think her life had been overrun by Sod's Law as of late. She also worried she over-reacted when Jez told her he was married. Most of their school-friends were in committed relationships, so it should have been no surprise that Jez found happiness. No, she knew her issue. It wasn't that Jez was gay, or that he was married. She didn't even mind that he was handsome. Alice couldn't stand the fact he'd forgotten about her.

One regret Alice carried around since she was sixteen had been leaving him at the cinema, and it turned out he didn't even remember her. Worse still, her leaving sent him straight into the arms of his future husband. If she hadn't stood him up, Jez wouldn't have kissed his first boy. At least, that was what she was telling herself.

Alice needed time away from her thoughts. She collected her keys and left the cottage.

Marsden's General Store didn't like to be called a corner shop. Sandra Marsden ran the place with her daughter, Indigo. A family business. The sort of business that passes down through the generations due to sheer bloody-mindedness rather than any wish to work in retail.

The place reeked of sawdust.

Sandra was renowned for a rebellious phase she went through as a teenager that had sent her to Warwick to practise Buddhism. She returned under something of a cloud when she tried to create a splinter group but ended up pregnant after burning down the YMCA.

She'd always been something of the contrarian – a rebel, a hipster of the disco era.

Alice arrived to find herself being greeted by Sandra, resplendent in orange kaftan, fake tribal patterns from head to toe. 'Namaste,' Sandra said, bobbing her head.

'Is that even Buddhist?'

'No idea. But I think it has more flare than "good morning", don't you?' She went back to Sudoku and left Alice to her own devices.

The first thing Alice discovered on the shelves was dust. Tons of dust. Though the place was lit as dimly as

Dracula's basement, she could see the spirals of dust making their patterns above the canned goods.

Still, Alice was here for one reason only: to acquire Pinot Grigio.

She hadn't been there for five minutes, staring at the shelves of wine, thinking about overloaded food environments, when her mother appeared.

Alice heard her before she saw her, returning Sandra's 'namaste' and saying how nice it was to keep up with old traditions.

'Thanks Primrose,' Sandra said. 'I think your daughter's down the wine aisle. She looked a bit upset if you ask me, but then I've always been more in touch with other people's auras. It's how I knew about Martin Kemp.'

'What about Martin Kemp?'

'Do you know, I can't remember.'

And then Primrose was at Alice's side. 'Alice, love, what are you doing here?'

Alice wrapped her arms around her mother and held tight. She inhaled the scent of her coat, her Alien perfume and the breeze, that cold smell that gets into everything. She closed her eyes, savouring the warmth of her mother's body.

'I don't think I'm moving in today, Mum,' she said, her words muffled by Primrose's Barbour jacket.

'I think you're right.' Primrose rubbed Alice's back in the way of all mothers, a cure for everything from trapped wind to heartbreak.

'Did you hear about the body?'

'Mr Sterling? Yes. Badminton was cancelled because of Rebecca Page's last surgery.'

'Right?'

'I thought I'd come and help at the cottage.'

'Only I wasn't there?' Alice stepped out of the hug and brushed her hair away from her face.

'I saw the police, Al. I spoke to Marmaduke. We were coming down to see you when you left in something of a huff.'

'I didn't see you.'

'I shouldn't think you would. At the rate you drove, you'd have Lewis Hamilton quaking in his shoes.'

'You're not going to stop me buying Pinot Grigio, are you?'

'That would be a job for your father. I came to make sure you're all right.'

Alice took a bottle from the shelf. 'Good, because today is not the day to hold a family intervention.'

'You found a body, Al. It's understandable you'd need a drink.'

'It's not for shock, Mum. This isn't medicinal vino to calm the nerves.' Alice held the bottle close to her chest as though it were her firstborn.

'Then what is it?'

Thoughts windmilled through Alice's mind. The fact was, she was embarrassed. The events of the morning raced with one another, each vying to make her feel worse.

'This is supposed to be a fresh start – to get me away from Wren's Lea and Mrs Cameron's death. The first thing that happens? A dead body. A corpse! And not just any corpse but that of Mr Sterling, murdered.'

'You have to leave it up to the police.'

'I just mean that it doesn't look good for me, does it? Two dead OAPs.'

'When all this has calmed down you'll be able to focus on the cottage and doing it up.'

'Do you think if I'd let Marmaduke stay then Mr

Sterling would still be alive?'

'I think you're looking for an excuse to drink Pinot Grigio.'

'Mum,' she groaned.

'Mr Sterling has been murdered. It's a sad turn of events, but you can be maudlin or you can help the police to the best of your abilities.'

'Do you know, mother, sometimes you give good maternal advice?'

'I should hope so. I took an evening class.'

With that, they went to purchase Alice's Pinot Grigio and set off on their way back home.

Chapter Eight

Next day, after an evening of drinking – well, until her father came home – and consoling from her parents, Alice piled the bin bags into her car and took them to the charity shop. It was a somewhat laborious operation, requiring workmen's gloves, industrial strength bin liners, and a strong sense of self-worth.

Alice didn't know how long Marmaduke's trash had been stored in the living room, but the bags perished when she lifted them, littering the floor with their contents, filling the air with frays of black plastic. She gagged a few times during her endeavours, but although she almost vomited when she discovered that what she thought was a slipper was actually a slimy bowl of fungus, she persisted.

As did the odour.

She'd opened all the windows when she arrived, and still the awful scent of sweating bin bags blended with the sickly sweet of rotten bananas and aged takeaways to permeate the household.

Alice took these bags to the tip. She drove with all the windows down, would have stuck her head out if she could've, but soon enough, Marmaduke's trash was gone.

Now, she had to contend with everything else. As she'd gone along, she'd separated the items she thought others could find some use for. She wasn't adept at recycling, but she didn't want to ruin her carbon footprint because of an unkempt old man with cleanliness issues.

She also took down the curtains. Aunty Magdalena had never been one for interior design; indeed, the curtains were present for every one of her six marriages. They were a ratty, mustard yellow, as though designed by Colman's. Alice had always assumed they were a throwback to the seventies, a reminder to Aunty Magdalena that she'd once had a waistline.

Forty years later, they were in a bin bag, all set for the charity shop.

Once more, Alice filled the car. This time, she set off towards Partridge Mews town centre.

There was still a police presence outside Arthur's house. Crime scene tape beribboned the hedges and stone walls. It could have been a scene from Midsomer Murders. Coroners ferreted about the property like astronauts in paper uniforms.

Alice had expected more people. She supposed the local constabulary didn't have as much money as television would have her believe.

The Partridge Mews Gazette had shared the news of Arthur's murder the previous evening. Luckily, they'd left Alice's name out of the article. She didn't think folk would think too kindly of a woman connected to the deaths of two OAPs.

Her drive into town was uneventful. She pulled up in front of the charity shop, cutting off Jeremy Vine mid-rant.

The East Cheshire Relief Fund for the Bewildered Elderly had prime position in the town centre, as did several other charity shops. Since her youth, Alice had seen the chain stores and independent shops close, leaving a whole host of charity shops and restaurants to rise in their place. She'd never really given it much thought until she'd had to drive to Poynton to buy an outfit for a wedding.

At least the place didn't smell like her childhood memories of charity shops, all cigarettes and ammonia. Sure, there was a hint of must in the air that could have been either the antique wardrobe in the middle of the shop or the gaggle of older ladies gossiping by the pound rail. That always seemed to be a guaranteed staple at charity shops: a gaggle of older ladies gossiping by the pound rail. Older men tended to congregate in libraries and allotments, out of the way and quiet, but the women owned their spot, glared at anyone who sought to get past, dared them to eavesdrop.

These were also the only women in the shop. Nobody stood at the till, guarding the display cabinet full of jewellery. A mass of bric-a-brac sat in the window, unsupervised, fit for the taking. Carlton ware stood beside Russell and Bromley shoes, more expensive than a holiday to Portugal. She understood they were a charity, but even high-class escorts sometimes gave it away on the cheap.

Alice had no choice but to approach the women. They surrounded the pound rail like a modern-day coven, all tight perms and Estée Lauder. They, each of them, were the very essence of smart casual, in their M&S tops and pleated trousers, creases so sharp they'd shame an accountant.

One of the women, clearly taking charge, took one

step forward to greet Alice. She had a false smile stamped against her face, her eyes giving the impression that all customers were unwelcome. 'Can I help you?' she asked, her voice high-pitched and breathy, like a hoover with a penny caught in its pipe.

'I have a car-load of bags to donate,' Alice said, feeling as though she was facing Partridge Mews's very own answer to Smaug.

The woman pursed her lips, the wrinkles spider-webbing around her mouth. 'Are you able to carry it all yourself, or should I fetch someone from the back room?'

Alice knew the answer immediately. 'I can bring them in myself, no bother.'

The smile again. 'Good. Well, I'll just nip through and let them know to expect you.'

Alice nodded and began the back and forth to her car. She heaved the bags with all the enthusiasm of a pack mule, questioning just why she'd filled the bags so much. She hadn't even looked at some of the stuff – just packed it into the bags and hoped for the best.

On her third trip, a man about her age appeared beside her. He was thin, lanky, and looked so unsure of himself that he reminded Alice of a new-born foal. 'Can I help at all?' he asked, his voice ropey, each word practically a different pitch.

'That'd be great, yeah.'

He leaned into the car and grabbed a few bags at once. This man clearly appreciated Lynx deodorant. He'd sprayed himself so liberally that Alice could taste it. As he leaned, his shirt rode up to reveal the waistband of his underwear. Sure, they might have looked like Calvin Klein, but Primark? No wonder he was so unsure of himself.

Alice followed him through to the back room to deposit her bags. A squat, dumpy-looking woman had already started sorting her donations.

'Found a friend have we, Martin?'

'Just thought I'd help carry some bags.'

'He's very chivalrous, is our Martin.'

Alice nodded, then pointed at the door. 'There aren't many more, I can probably bring them myself.' She sped away before she heard the woman's next comment, but it was enough to elicit a 'give over, Bev' from Martin.

She thought she'd shook him off, left the weird charity shop people to their own devices, but Martin came to the side of her car again moments later. 'Sorry about that,' he said, running a hand through his shaggy hair, looking like some sort of dishevelled Dulux dog.

'It's fine,' Alice said, 'I just want to–'

Bev screamed.

A high-pitched wail as theatrical as *Les Misérables* cut Alice off mid-sentence.

Martin flew back inside like a whippet.

Alice followed him into the back room, alongside the older ladies.

Bev stood at the table holding a large, cracked ornament, somewhat canine in appearance. Sure, it could be seen as scary, but Alice guessed it wasn't the ornament that had caused Bev to wail like a banshee. No, the reason she'd screamed was the dried blood covering the thing, and, on the base, what Alice could only assume was brain matter.

'Well, that doesn't look good,' Alice said.

Chapter Nine

Once Alice left the police station, she was well and truly shattered. She'd provided a statement saying she hadn't known what was in the bags. She couldn't be sure they were happy with her, but at least now they had a possible murder weapon. They'd taken Alice's fingerprints, in any case.

Luckily, it wasn't too far to her car.

She drove back to the cottage under police investigation, with the knowledge she could never return to the East Cheshire Relief Fund for the Bewildered Elderly. A shame, considering it was the only charity shop in Partridge Mews where you could park outside.

Alice arrived to find Marmaduke in the living room. He had a can of John Smiths in his hand and a wry smile on his face that Alice usually associated with night club weirdoes who got too handsy. He'd clearly been drinking for a while. The room stank of cheap beer and empty promises. There were also a few cans around his feet.

'Make yourself at home,' he said, a drunken drawl to his voice. 'There's wine in the fridge.'

'I know. It's my wine.'

He shook his head. 'Not that cheap rubbish from Marsden's. I bought it for you.'

Alice quirked an eyebrow as she meandered towards the kitchen. True enough, Marmaduke had purchased a bottle of wine. She poured herself a large measure and returned to the living room. She sat in the armchair across from him, beside the window.

'So, found yourself a murder weapon, did you?'

Alice held up her index finger to silence him. She kicked off her shoes and swilled the wine around her glass before taking a long slug. It tasted sweet and smooth as it travelled down her throat, and comfortingly cold. She looked Marmaduke dead in the eye and said, 'That's good. Now, forgetting you broke into my house, how do you know about the murder weapon?'

'I used to be in the police.'

'Not an answer.'

'The women of Partridge Mews are renowned gossips. By the time I'd found out about the discovery, you were accused of murder, close to being sent down after the police linked Arthur's death to that Cameron woman.'

She nodded. 'Makes sense.'

'What're you thinking?'

'I was going to come home, have a bath, and scream into my pillow.'

'All that?'

Alice crossed her legs beneath her on the chair, looking set to meditate. She breathed deeply and said, 'What do you know about the murder?'

Marmaduke shifted his gaze, refusing to acknowledge her. He passed his beer between his hands, allowing silence to fill the room.

Alice drank her wine and checked her nails, then scraped some dirt from the index finger. Birds chirruped outside. Cars passed by. One of the neighbours had Granada Reports on much too loud, Lucy and Tony booming out news – someone had slipped on a quiche in Waitrose and chosen to sue, not because it shouldn't have happened but because they were vegan and the moral implications of quiche had caused them to seek behavioural therapy.

Marmaduke remained silent.

Alice finished her wine, returned to the kitchen and came back with the bottle. 'Honestly, the amount of alcohol I've consumed in the last few weeks? It's no wonder people are accusing me of bumping off old folk.'

'They don't really think that.'

'They've already started gossiping. Now tell me what you know.'

He sighed.

'Is this the way you go about all conversations? Shutting up and refusing to answer any questions? Because it doesn't give you the mysterious allure of Batman, it just makes you look a right old–'

'All right,' he said. 'I can tell you.'

'I know you can, so speak.'

'I already told you about Arthur's investigation.'

'You did. He was snooping around town and annoyed a ton of folk. I suppose that means the police will have to track down all the people he spoke to and question them.'

'Why ask questions if you're going to answer yourself?'

'Need I remind you that you broke in?'

'I brought wine.'

'Touché.'

They took a moment to admire their respective drinks, sipping and slurping in equal measure.

'Anyway,' Marmaduke said, 'the police would interview Arthur's witnesses, but his notebook is missing.'

'His notebook?'

'Yup. Arthur kept all his notes in a cheap Sainsbury's exercise book. We've seen it, and now it's missing.'

'And it's important that we find the notebook?'

'We?'

'Come on, Duke. I found the body. You're a former detective. It stands to reason we should put our heads together and solve the thing.'

'How much wine have you had?'

Alice thought about this for a moment. She supposed she'd had a fair amount on an empty stomach. She'd declined all offers of refreshments at the station in case it could be seen as an admission of guilt, as though the police would look at her jail cell cheese sandwich and say to one another, 'Oh, look at her, she's eating to get used to the taste of prison food.' They'd have her in front of the judge before she'd had chance to digest it.

She had the heavy head associated with tipsiness, that familiar ache above her ears. Maybe choosing to man her own murder investigation was a mistake, but she had this urge to prove to the world that she didn't despise the older generations. She hadn't meant to lose her job, nor had she wanted to contribute to the death of Mrs Cameron, no matter what people claimed.

Alice had always wanted to make a difference.

At school, she'd organised penny trails and nonuniform days for various charities, whatever felt most important to her at the time. She'd spent her life fighting feelings of worthlessness, and now, with a murder at her door, she'd found the opportunity to put those feelings to bed.

Alice sat up straight, selfishly serious. 'You had me take photos, Duke. You must have wanted some involvement.'

He looked uneasy again. 'Delete them. I'm not sure it's the best idea anymore.'

'I doubted it. You called it freelancing.'

'Before I knew the murderer had been in your cottage, Alice. Before I understood how serious things were.'

'You were a detective.'

'And now I'm retired.'

Alice didn't understand Marmaduke's change of heart. She stared at him. There were dark circles under his eyes. He hadn't brushed his hair.

'It's only been a day. You lost a friend – that's got to be difficult – but yesterday you wanted to know who'd done Arthur wrong. Today, you broke in because I found the murder weapon, so what did I say to change your mind?'

'If you're so excited to be a detective, why don't you share your leads with me?' He dropped his empty can to the floor, challenging her.

Alice had an answer on the tip of her tongue. 'There's a man called Ronnie. I saw him arguing with Mr Sterling yesterday morning.'

Marmaduke stopped stock still for a moment. 'Ronnie Butterworth?'

Alice shrugged. 'Could be. If that's a name you associate with Mr Sterling.'

'All right. What do you suggest?'

'We sober up and go see him in the morning.'

Marmaduke bowed his head. 'We'll see.'

Chapter Ten

Alice picked Marmaduke up the next day. He lived in a semi-detached house on Micawber Lane. The house could barely be seen beneath its greenery – every inch was being choked by heavy mounds of ivy. It spread across the white concrete, gone wild, shrouding the windows, pilfering brickwork. The front lawn looked as though it could belong to Steptoe and Son; old wheelbarrow tyres, broken machinery, and car parts filled the lawn.

It made no sense. Marmaduke had made such a good job of Aunty Magdalena's cottage. Had he transferred all her ivy to his own property?

Alice pressed her car horn, refusing to set foot in what was left of his garden.

After a few minutes of inactivity, she pressed the horn again, to little avail.

Marmaduke didn't appear.

Alice groaned, head in hands. Passersby looked in at the disenchanted brunette. Perhaps they recognised her as the girl connected to the deaths of two OAPs in Partridge Mews; and, since this morning, an assault on Mr Roger Valentine.

She'd woken up and checked her phone to find a plethora of messages from her family and friends. Primrose told her to look at Facebook. She did. The headline branded itself on her eyelids: *Niece Clobbers Uncle in Cottage Con Row.* The article discussed how she'd systematically preyed on Aunty Magdalena and tricked her into signing the cottage over. It also said that when Roger, the hero of the piece, confronted her, she'd assaulted him. His wife didn't say anything explicitly about Alice killing Mrs Cameron and Mr Sterling, but it was heavily implied. Even the Gazette mentioned that she'd been questioned by police and that although she'd been released, the murder hadn't been solved.

Alice made the mistake of scrolling through the comments. She was forty-three messages deep: former school-friends tagging one another, saying they couldn't believe it, how they'd always known she was a bad 'un, and then came Eloise Pidgeon. They'd never been friends at school. Alice thought she'd have got over their feud now they were both adults, but no. Eloise went into a long spiel about how it didn't surprise her as Alice proved at school the measure of her ruthlessness, how due to Alice she failed her English GCSE and subsequently missed out on a career as a high-flying beauty therapist.

What Eloise failed to mention was that she plagiarised all her essays from her older brother, and when Alice found out she informed the head of English, who checked and realised the truth. He gave Eloise the opportunity to redo her coursework, but Eloise decided that would be an admission of guilt and accepted the U grade. And now the chance to call Alice a murderer had come along and she gloried in it, liking abusive and defamatory comments, sharing and tagging to her heart's content.

Alice switched off notifications on her phone and got herself ready for the day.

Only to arrive at Marmaduke's and find him ignoring her.

She had no choice. She'd have to go inside and get him.

He'd been a little worse for wear when he'd left. They'd continued drinking until eight in the evening, though Alice switched to coffee – decaff with three sugars, despite the late hour. Marmaduke continued on the beer, seemingly pulling more cans out of his backside.

Now he wasn't responding to Alice. She got out of the car and made her way over to the garden gate, a waist-high thing that had been green at some point. The hinges were broken, the wood was cracked and panels were missing; like most other things to do with Marmaduke, it had fallen into disrepair.

Marmaduke grew dandelions in his garden. They festered, poking their heads out of every spare patch of grass. As for the thin, stone path, what hadn't been smothered by moss was cracked, slabs upended and tossed aside to reveal the soil and the worms, woodlice and earwigs that called it home. Alice crept slowly towards the front door, which looked as shabby as the rest of the place.

The door was open.

Alice smiled and shook her head. Marmaduke had broken into her cottage, left it in a style to which he was accustomed, and now she had a chance to return the favour.

She pushed the door open and recoiled. The odour he'd made at her cottage was nothing compared to the rancid stench that attacked Alice's nostrils as she entered the house. She needed Febreze – heck, she needed to find a couple of Glade air fresheners and to pack them into her nostrils.

Marmaduke was a hoarder. He could stock a charity shop for months from the contents of his hall alone.

'Duke,' Alice called, 'I can't imagine the WI will be happy with the state of your garden.'

Sunlight struck the dust motes in the air. Everything was coated in thick brown dust and cobwebs – wherever she looked, cobwebs. Even the photos hanging on the wall were lost behind curtains of dust.

'Duke?'

Still no answer. She brushed past the bin bags, aware of the state they made of her jeans. Her nose itched. There was a tickle in the back of her throat, and she hoped beyond hope there wasn't anything catching. It would be just her luck to catch bubonic plague from Marmaduke's rubbish.

'I swear, if you're still asleep, I'll kill you.' Alice winced. 'Probably not the best thing to say, Al.'

She stuck her head around the corner of the first door she met. The living room. At least, what she thought was the living room. It was difficult to tell when every inch of space was occupied by bin bags and cardboard boxes.

Alice's heart leapt into her throat. She clutched the door jamb, eyes on the inanimate figure sprawled atop the clutter like a great offering to the patron saint of dust collectors. A blue glow covered him, some ethereal combination of sun and shabby curtains.

'Duke?' The name eked from between her lips, little more than a squeak. She saw the path he must have made before collapsing. She followed this path now, eyes on his chest, watching for a rise and fall, the heaving breaths of a practised wheezer.

He didn't make a sound.

Alice stood over him.

His wrinkled skin seemed paler, but that could've been the light. He didn't look peaceful. He looked like he'd fought nine rounds with arthritis, his crooked body spread-eagled into shapes a contortionist would be proud of.

Alice turned around and opened the curtains. She shivered, her body tense, like when you're snooping through someone's things, knowing they could walk in at any moment.

These windows held some shadow from the ivy but the sun shone through, almost blinding as it crafted shadow puppets from sycamore trees.

There was a groan behind her.

Alice gasped. She spun around to see the great, burly form of Marmaduke Featherstone awakening. She did what any other person would do in the situation.

She slapped him.

Once, then once more for good measure. 'I thought you were dead,' she exclaimed, the rush of relief bringing colour to her cheeks.

'What time?' he said, rubbing his cheeks and shifting himself about so he looked like a beached whale. If he moved a leg, the bin bags would slide into the boxes, they'd spill onto a sofa that seemed to be a repository for coats, jumpers and something neon pink that Alice only hoped wasn't Duke's.

'Do you want a hand?'

'No, I want to stay here practising my breast stroke.' His voice was a growl.

'You're in no position to talk dirty to me, Duke.'

'Just help me up before I wet myself.'

It took some heaving, some toing and froing, and the destruction of a few boxes to get Marmaduke on his feet. Once he'd stood up, he toddled off to perform the necessaries, leaving Alice alone, feeling a right lemon.

She idled around, felt the satisfaction of running her finger through thick dust. It left a clear line on the mahogany sideboard, but she imagined it would be covered again soon enough.

There were photographs on the sideboard in old frames. Some were water damaged, with cracked or missing glass. Holiday snaps, school photos, candid family pictures taken somewhere else – not Partridge Mews, and certainly not people Alice had ever seen before. She could tell the photos were old from the clothes, all denim and perms and a young girl in a Tiswas t-shirt.

The girl appeared in nearly all the photos, from baby pictures up to a high school disco and then nothing. They ended abruptly with the image of a blonde teenager, hair crimped with blue clip-on highlights. Her smile revealed braces. She looked like every child of the nineties in her tie-dye shirt, flared jeans and glitter platforms; an homage to the ever-popular Spice Girls.

Could this be Duke's daughter?

Maybe all the bin bags were something to do with her. Alice glanced over at the garments leaking from the hoard. She inched her way back across the room, careful in case Duke knew the exact position of each and every box. She picked up a dress between pincered fingers. Dust scattered from the crumples and creases as though she were excavating Tutankhamun's wardrobe. An odour of damp must blew in her face like an attack from an over-zealous perfume seller. The dress was a size eight, black with sequins.

'You can put that down for a start.'

Alice bolted upright. She'd been paying close attention to the seams, counting sequins, and hadn't given any thought to the looming shadow in the doorway. She placed the dress back on top of the bags and met his gaze.

He didn't look angry; his eyes weren't glazed with the wild intensity of a caught transvestite.

Alice clasped her hands together, unsure what else to do with them. She knew she ought to speak, to break the silence, but she couldn't come up with any reasons for snooping.

'I'm sorry, Duke, it just caught my eye and—'

'I imagine Primrose taught you to look with your eyes and not your hands.' Marmaduke sighed. He gripped his hair in his right hand, eyes weary, barely wide – bright blue lights in the caverns of his wrinkles.

'Do you want me to make a brew?' Alice asked.

Marmaduke looked gone out, staring into space in his own private, worrisome world. 'I'm going to get changed. Don't touch anything else.'

'Shall I wait in the car?'

'If it'll stop you rifling through my things, then yes.'

Nearly twenty minutes later, he appeared at the front door like some great waif in some ragged jacket with more patches than pockets. She didn't know what had happened to the duffel coat. He moved slowly, gingerly towards the car, his trousers scuffing on the stones and soil.

He was silent as he climbed into the car. This wasn't the silence Primrose used to get Alice to reveal secrets. This was an unanswerable silence, the silence of a man who's been hurt and who doesn't know how to verbalise it.

'Duke,' Alice said, eager to make things right.

He held up his hand to cut her off before she could begin. 'We need to go see Ronnie, you said. Let's go see Ronnie.'

'Where does he live?'

Marmaduke bristled for a moment. He stopped himself from excreting the rant he clearly had waiting on the tip of his tongue and said, 'Brook Farm on the Wren's Lea Road. You must have driven past it hundreds of times.'

Alice nodded and kept quiet. Marmaduke definitely wasn't one for conversation. In fact, he didn't speak for the entire journey. She expected him to object as she switched on the radio – lord knew she needed the company – but he said nothing as Adele's *Hometown Glory* came blaring from the speakers.

They made it in a quarter of an hour. A rough stone track led towards the farm. Sheep gambolled about the fields, blarting and bleating like a chorus of badly-played bagpipes.

The car trundled past. Stones crunched beneath the wheels and shot darts at the paintwork.

Marmaduke remained silent.

'You know, Duke, you spend an awful amount of time not saying anything.'

He shrugged. 'I listened to my mother is all. If there's nowt nice to say, I'd sooner say nowt.'

'Says the man who called my Aunty Magdalena's cottage a doss house.'

'I was provoked.'

'By who?'

'You insulted my character.'

'You filled the place with bin bags.'

'You threw them out, didn't you?'

'Someone hid the murder weapon in them.'

'Well it wasn't me.'

'How could it be? That would mean shifting your backside.'

They pulled into the yard. Alice thought her suspension would be grateful for the change of terrain. Here, the farmer had tarmacked, though it did seem pointless considering you knackered your car enough beforehand. Then Alice saw it: another track, perfectly flat, leading off in the opposite direction. She turned on Marmaduke, as angry as a wasp in a milk bottle. 'Why didn't you tell me about the other entrance?'

He shrugged again, chin on his chest. 'Doesn't matter. We're here, aren't we?'

'Let's just go speak to Ronnie.'

They both got out of the car. Marmaduke huffed and puffed all the way to his feet. 'Do I have to remind you that I didn't want you getting involved?' he said.

'Yesterday, maybe, but you involved me when you had me take photographs of a corpse.'

'He was my friend.'

'That's no excuse. When a friend dies, your first thought shouldn't be "let's get a picture of his bludgeoned body as a memento".' Alice slammed her car door shut and turned around, her back against it. She breathed deep.

'You know, you can be incredibly hurtful at times.'

'And you can be an insufferable old twerp.' She folded her arms. She felt the heat rising to her cheeks, imagined the mottled red skin like luncheon meat, a veritable sign she'd let him get to her again. He just had this way about him that infuriated her. It was in his mannerisms and his words, and it drove her around the twist.

Yet in the back of her mind, she couldn't escape her mother's words. If Primrose were to see the way Alice treated Marmaduke, she'd take her aside and tell her she was being disrespectful, that she didn't know the true measure of Duke's character, didn't know what caused a man to choose to live in such a way.

Maybe she'd never been a good social worker after all.

Alice slumped against her car, almost scorching her back in the process. It was too hot for May. On the drive up, she'd seen people in woolly jumpers and others in shorts, as though the town couldn't decide if it were Malta or Antarctica. It was neither. It was a small, northern town in England, more likely to trust a barometer over a meteorologist.

Alice hoped she could blame her attitude on the heat. She faced him, conjuring an apologetic smile, a cross between a dog caught with its head in the toilet and Lindsay Lohan, and said, 'Look, Duke, I'm sorry I went snooping through your things. I shouldn't have done that.'

'Well I'm glad you're showing some common sense.'

Alice offered a curt nod. 'Right. Shall we go and speak to Ronnie?'

'We can't very well stand around here kissing each other's backsides.'

Alice turned on her heel and headed towards the farmhouse. She crossed the path between two small vegetable patches.

There was no one home. Alice knocked on the front door and peeked through the windows to find nothing. No person, no creature in sight – she'd at least expected a sheepdog of some sort, something to bound out and muddy her jeans.

'We should try the shop,' she said, turning back to Duke.

He stood in the doorway of the small annexe, crunching an apple. 'Should we?'

'I hope you paid for that.'

'Want one?' He tossed it over before she could answer.

She rubbed it on her top and bit a large chunk. 'Any other ideas?' she asked, between bites.

'Let's have a look round. If he's not here, we'll leave it.'

It didn't take long to find Ronnie. The two of them had only just rounded the corner of the farm shop when they came across him – or rather, his body.

Alice dropped her apple and stared at him, open-mouthed.

Ronnie hung from the rafters of the shippon, noose around his neck. Flies feasted on his flesh, buzzing around him in great swarms of fizzing blackness. They crawled into his mouth and lay dead on the floor beneath him.

Alice felt all emotion flee her body. Nausea took hold in an instant and, before she knew it, she vomited over the nearest drystone wall, chunks of apple reminding her that she and Marmaduke had just stolen from a dead man.

Chapter Eleven

Once again, Alice found herself escorted home by Jez. She'd left Marmaduke to telephone the police while she went and hid in the car, unable to spend any longer looking at Ronnie Butterworth's corpse. Not only that, but Alice also wondered what people would say now she was connected to the deaths of four OAPs. Granted, Aunty Magdalena died in Madeira of heart problems, but Alice was certain they'd try to pin it on her. The police would see they'd FaceTimed on the morning of her death and the mere stress of seeing Alice's ugly mug was enough to kill off Aunty Magdalena.

These were just a few of Alice's thoughts as Jez drove her home. Clive said he'd give Marmaduke a lift.

As soon as they arrived back at the cottage, Alice was in the kitchen. She hurriedly searched the cupboards, grabbing at tins, bags and assorted packages in her quest.

'What the heck are you doing?' Jez asked.

She stopped for a moment, looked him dead in the eye, and said, 'I need to bake a cake.'

'Can't it wait? I have to ask you a few questions,

remember?'

'When I'm stressed, I bake.' She crouched beside a lower cupboard, hiding behind the door.

'You bake?'

'Pies, pastries, cakes, cookies. I gained a stone revising for my A-Levels.'

A flash of realisation struck Jez in the face. 'That's what that was. We all thought you were pregnant.'

Alice stood up, a manky baking tin in her hands. 'Who's "we"?'

Jez averted his eyes from Alice's fiery gaze. 'The English Language class. Amanda Sutcliffe bet £20.00 you'd call the baby "Cullen".'

Alice looked set to bake Jez into a pie. Her face was so contorted with fury that she could've been mistaken for a dried apricot. 'Why Cullen?'

'You know, because of your *Twilight* phase.'

'Everyone had a *Twilight* phase. It was part of the cultural zeitgeist.'

Jez shrugged. 'I suppose I did have a bit of a thing for Taylor Lautner.'

'As did every other teenager of the time.' The strain in Alice's neck subsided as she started to calm down. She set the baking tin on the counter and said, 'Did you see the woman with the *Twilight* back tattoo.'

'The one with every character?'

Alice nodded. 'She paid thousands of dollars for that. Honestly, all that money for Kristen Stewart on your back – even the Mona Lisa cracked a smile every now and then.'

'Are you saying all this to deflect from my questions about Mr Butterworth?'

Alice switched on the kettle. 'Would you like a brew?'

A few minutes later, they sat in the living room with their drinks while Jez went through his questions. Alice told him how she and Marmaduke had gone to speak to Ronnie about Arthur's murder, only to find a corpse.

'Was it suicide?' she asked, immediately condemning her own morbid curiosity.

Jez shrugged and bit the end of his pen. 'You really shouldn't be conducting your own investigation, Alice. It's not only dangerous, it's also illegal.'

'Just say I took Duke to buy some apples, then.'

Jez sighed at this and shook his head, but he still had a smile on his face. 'Besides, why visit Ronnie? What has he got to do with anything?'

'I saw him arguing with Arthur the morning he was murdered.'

She'd piqued his interest, she could tell. His back was straight, eyes alert, like a dog after leftovers. His eyes had that inquisitive look that men get when they're trying to tell if you're wearing any underwear. He chewed his cheek, mulling something over. He'd disappeared into some sort of reverie, and Alice had no choice but to watch him and sup at her tea.

'I don't think it was Arthur,' he said, a few minutes later.

Alice put her phone down. She'd been checking celebrity news and gossip – apparently Cheryl Cole was having relationship troubles again. To be honest, Alice had forgotten Jez was there. He was so quiet, he could've been a potted plant. She said, 'Do you know, Jeremy–'

'It's Jez.'

'Jez, I knew you were going to say that.'

'Say what?'

'About it not being Arthur.'

'How did you know?'

'You became very interested in my cleavage, and considering you're in a committed relationship with a man, you'd either realised it wasn't Arthur or made a baffling lifestyle choice.'

'Sorry.'

She grinned at him. 'I'm just glad you were thinking about Arthur.'

'Anyway, I think you saw Ronnie arguing with Bertram – Arthur's brother.'

'Why?'

'Because if our coroner knows her stuff then Arthur had been dead for a fair few hours when you found him.'

'Why would they be arguing?'

Jez shrugged. 'I have an idea, but this is police business, Alice. It's not for you to worry about.'

'I get that, but I still want to know.'

'You know we're not incompetent. We have resources and–'

'Jez, I found two bodies and someone left a possible murder weapon in my recently-inherited cottage. I'm going to be part of your investigation whatever happens.'

'I just don't want you going about playing Miss Marple.'

'Are you calling me old?'

Jez clammed up. He blinked a few times, uncertain how best to proceed. He'd always been the same at school. Alice recalled a Maths class when Mr Gainsborough had asked Jez for an answer from their homework – homework he'd been copying from Scott McEwan. He froze like a badger on a football pitch and came up with some story about his revision being stolen by a swan in the park. As they sat there, she remembered the glazed look in his eyes, his flushed, red neck, and, 'You fancied Mr Gainsborough?' erupted from her lips before she had a chance to stifle it.

Shock caused Jez to sink further back into the sofa, as though he hoped the cushions would absorb him. 'I don't know what you're talking about.'

Alice simmered down. 'Sorry. I just remembered his class. You went all red and, well, you looked at him.'

'Don't pretend you never fancied a teacher.'

'Of course I did, everyone does. It's high school.' Alice grinned bigger than a Cheshire cat. 'Anyway, seriously, why would Ronnie argue with Mr Sterling's brother?'

'I told you, I–'

'Was it the older man thing that did it for you?'

'We're not doing this, Alice. I'm here to ask you questions, not to talk about Mr Gainsborough.' His eyes widened so much that they looked set to fall out of his head.

'This is what friends do, Jez. They tease each other about their crushes.'

'But we're not friends. Yes, we went to school together, but we haven't seen each other in seven years.'

He had a point. Sure, she was Facebook friends with an old profile of his, but that just meant she could see what he looked like in 2010. She hadn't even known he was married. 'You're right. Look, let's forget I said anything. Go ahead, ask me your questions.'

'I thought you wanted to know why Ronnie would be arguing with Bertram.'

'I do, but then I upset you and thought it best to leave things.'

'They could've been arguing about any number of

things. I wonder if it's something to do with Arthur's investigation into Christopher Partridge's death. Originally, the plan had been for a few more officers to be patrolling the grounds, but they were called out to an armed robbery in town.'

'Why did they leave Arthur behind?'

Jez slurped his drink and smacked his lips together. 'No idea. Either way, when they get to the jewellers, there's no sign of any robbery but they find Ronnie's gun.'

'But they didn't find Ronnie?'

Jez shook his head and leaned forward. 'Witnesses said they saw Ronnie at Greenfields, the assumption being that he faked the robbery to murder the heir.'

'Was he charged?'

'He claimed the gun had been stolen. Christopher's sister Clementine came forward in support of Ronnie saying there was no reason to believe he'd killed Christopher. Ronnie was cleared and left town. He only came back when his father died.'

'And you think Arthur's investigation might have upset him?'

'If someone accused you of murder, how would you react?'

Alice stifled a laugh on the back of her hand, thinking about how the papers had painted her recently. 'We really don't know each other, do we?'

Chapter Twelve

That evening, Alice returned to her parents' house for tea. She'd only moved out two days earlier – two days and two corpses. If this were some sort of millennial housewarming trend, she wanted no part of it. As if she hadn't had enough of death recently. What with the deaths of Aunty Magdalena and Mrs Cameron, Alice thought she was well above her yearly quota.

Alice barely knew Arthur Sterling. She'd had a crush on his grandson back in the day, had been known to request picnics on Aunty Magdalena's front garden just for the chance to watch Luke mow his grandfather's lawn, but she only knew Arthur enough to recognise him at the supermarket. As for Ronnie Butterworth, she didn't know he existed until she caught him arguing with Arthur's brother.

She didn't know them, and yet she felt responsible for them. Some hidden part of her conscience curdled within her, fermenting, until she feared she had no choice but to try and help figure out just what had happened.

Although she did wonder if that was the Pinot Grigio. As soon as she'd hung her coat on the hook,

Primrose appeared with a large glass of the glorious nectar.

'I really shouldn't,' she'd said, following her mother into the kitchen, with no intention of exchanging her alcohol for water.

Primrose clearly agreed because she said, 'You're not leaving me to drink on my own, Al. What do I always tell you? Drinking alone is alcoholism, drinking together is…'

'Therapy.' Alice clinked her glass against her mother's, having given her the answer she wanted. 'Where's Dad?'

Primrose waved a hand through the air, as though planning to conjure him from the ether. 'He's only gone and got himself a new helmet camera, hasn't he?'

'You already told me that, and you still haven't told me where he is.'

'Where is he usually?'

'The front room?'

Primrose glugged her wine and nodded, looking somewhat like a pelican. She swallowed. 'Got it in one.'

'What's for tea?'

'Indian. Your father says he's going to pick it up, but I imagine he's busy polishing his handlebars.'

Alice snorted into her glass. 'Mum!'

'Don't blame me for your dirty mind, that comes from your father's side of the family. Look at your Aunty Magdalena, she knew her way around a double-entendre.'

Alice drew swirls in the condensation of her glass. 'Not to be funny, but have you and Dad had a row?'

Primrose tried to shrug it off but ended up looking like a slug who'd just been salted. 'It was something of nothing. I knew what I was getting into when I married a keen cyclist.'

'What's that got to do with anything?'

'Oh, it doesn't matter. We'll be fine. He'll continue to make ridiculous decisions without talking them through with me, and I'll book another holiday without asking. Before you know it, we'll be in scorching hot Llandudno, and he'll have saddle burns like cow pats on his backside.'

Alice allowed herself a few moments to stare agog at Primrose before saying, 'Do you want me to speak to him?'

'I've told you before that it's not your place to settle parental disputes. Frankly, I'm appalled I spoke so candidly to you.'

'You've been reading parenting manuals again, haven't you?'

Primrose looked shiftily around the kitchen, unsure where to settle her gaze. 'I just like to keep abreast of modern parenting techniques.'

'I'm twenty-five.'

'Does that mean I stop being your parent?'

'It means the damage has been done. There's nothing you can do to make me a better member of society.'

'Now, I don't believe that at all.'

They heard a door open down the hall. Norman entered the kitchen. 'I thought I'd just nip out and get some tea.'

Primrose handed him his car keys. 'That's one of your better ideas this evening.'

'It's a charity bike ride, Prim.'

'That will last for a month. What the devil am I expected to do with myself?'

'Do I need to mention Nepal again?'

Primrose looked elsewhere. 'That was different. It was years ago.'

'What about Nepal?' Alice asked.

Norman didn't look angry, he looked hurt. A vein on his neck pulsed like a worm beneath his skin. 'When you were eighteen months old–'

'Oh, it's that story,' Alice said, realisation kicking in. It was one of her parents' favourite sticking points. When Alice was eighteen months old, Primrose decided to go and do some charity work in Nepal, building houses, feeding folk, and doing everything in her power to improve her spiritual health. This meant leaving Norman and Alice in Wren's Lea – an act that, whilst he claimed to have forgiven it, Norman brought up during most arguments, most bafflingly when they went to buy Alice's prom dress and he got upset over bare shoulders.

And now he'd brought it up again, ostensibly due to a charity bike ride. 'It's exactly the same situation.'

'It's not that, Dad,' Alice said. 'I just thought you had some new scandal to add to the tale.'

'No, Al, your father has clearly waited twenty-five years to exact his revenge.'

Norman gawped at Primrose. 'I'm going to pick up tea.'

He left his wife and daughter in the silent kitchen. Alice checked her reflection in a pan lid as Primrose stared after her husband. 'Well, I clearly take after you when it comes to upsetting men,' Alice said.

Primrose blinked for a few moments, oblivious. Once her reverie was broken, she said, 'What did you say, love?'

Alice repeated herself.

'What do you mean?'

'I went to Duke's today – I thought he was dead. He was in a room filled with bin bags. I didn't realise he's such a hoarder. Anyway, he went off to get changed and I got curious and started looking at the things in one of the bin bags. It was crammed full of ladies' clothes. At first, I thought he might be gender-fluid, but there were these pictures of this girl.'

'That'll be Joanna,' Primrose said.

'And who's she?'

'His niece. She went missing years ago. Duke was still on the force then. He put all his efforts into finding her, but nothing.'

'How come I never heard about it?'

'You have to imagine it from a parent's perspective. A young girl goes missing and you begin to worry that your child will be next. She just vanished, Alice. No letter. No sign if she'd been kidnapped or run away.' Primrose clenched the edge of the counter, jaw taut at the memory. 'We'd roam the streets at night, with search parties, police dogs, the works.'

'Who are her parents?'

'Andy and Seraphina Hollinshead.'

'Duke's parents had a thing for weird names, then?'

'They come from old money, it's one of those things.' Primrose finished her wine. 'Anyway, it's always going to eat away at Duke. He saw Joanna as the daughter he never had. He worshipped her.'

'And there's no knowing where she went?'

Primrose shrugged. 'It's got to be getting on for nearly twenty years, now. If she's still living, I'd like to think she'd at least have the heart to get in touch with her parents.'

'What if they're the reason she disappeared?'

This did it for Primrose. She visibly shuddered, eyes

closed, shoulders taut. 'Let's talk about something else, I can't bear thinking about it.'

'All right then. I found another dead man today.'

'Oh love, you don't have any luck, do you?'

They ended up refilling their glasses and wandering into the living room, where Alice told Primrose about finding Ronnie's body and Jez's subsequent interrogation.

Alice had grown used to the living room over time, but it was still unnerving to be surrounded by so many photos of herself. The living room was a veritable shrine to Alice. Primrose had even framed Alice's school certificates, including one dated October 1995 for successfully reciting the alphabet. Despite her penchant for joining every life improvement class Wren's Lea offered, Primrose could win awards for being supportive.

Primrose listened to Alice's tale and said, 'Well Ronnie's been going up to the Sterlings' farm for years.'

'What are you saying?'

'It's common knowledge, really. Ronnie was having an affair with Bertram's wife.'

'Do you think that's why they were arguing?'

Primrose thought for a moment. 'No. That's not an argument you have in a hardware store.'

'Did you know about the fake robbery?'

'Not at the time. Bear in mind I was three years old, but it all resurfaced when Ronnie came back.'

Alice rolled her eyes. 'Local gossip, I'm guessing.'

'No, love. Ronnie decided to ask his own questions. He was convinced someone tried to frame him and wanted to know who.'

'Do you think he got Arthur to help him out?'

'They're both dead. We'll never know.'

And there it was again, the feeling of responsibility. Alice knew her mother was right, that they couldn't ask dead men any questions, but she had a connection to them now. She'd help find out who killed Arthur and Ronnie Butterworth and by the time she finished with them, the murderer would be begging for the police.

Chapter Thirteen

When Duke rang a few days later, Alice was in a carpet shop. She'd stayed with her parents on the night of the takeaway, in the hope that her mere presence would cause them to drop their argument. It didn't. If anything, it made them worse. It began with Norman mentioning that he'd potty trained Alice, which led to Primrose saying he only did it because he couldn't stand dirty nappies. This descended into a great battle over everything her parents had ever done for her.

'I took her to baby yoga.' Norman.

'I taught her Tibetan meditation rituals.' Primrose.

'Irish dancing, violin lessons, guitar lessons, that introductory saxophone class.'

'She had a chest infection.'

'How was I to know she'd collapse?'

'It's a brass instrument. She wasn't going to play with her toes.'

'It was your idea. You kept harping on about how the saxophone was a typically masculine instrument and it would make you proud if Alice were to flip traditional roles.' This led to a somewhat breathless Norman, but whether that was the conversation or his tikka masala, no one could tell.

Not that it mattered, Primrose still had plenty to say on the matter. 'I'd been listening to Mrs Copeland, hadn't I? Besides, I thought Alice might have liked to learn the theme tune to *A Touch of Frost*, you know how much I like David Jason.' That much was true. Alice was eleven when Primrose had told her that should she ever hear the sound of *Only Fools and Horses* coming from her parents' bedroom, she should make herself scarce. There was many a time that Alice would get home from school and have to disappear to the park when she caught wind of *The Jolly Boy's Outing*.

The argument was far from over when Alice retired to her bedroom with a glass of milk and an onion bhaji. She was just closing the door when her father exclaimed, 'Well, I'm sorry I have a penis!'

Alice wasn't tired. Whilst she started well by Googling Christopher Partridge's murder, she soon found herself on Pinterest and Tumblr, scrolling through décor trends. There were a lot of flowers. Roses on white backgrounds, violets on white backgrounds, extremely bold peonies. Nothing she was really looking for. She scrolled through an endless stream of neutral-toned decorating ideas. Most designers painted everything beige and put a Jackson Pollock in the airing cupboard. There were pastel shades of blue, pink, and purple to appeal to the modern people who appreciated colour but wanted nothing to take their minds off avocado.

Eventually, Alice fell asleep.

Her parents had left when she woke the next morning, and her search began again. She was aware it wasn't the search she should be making, that procrastination was the thief of time, but surely finding two corpses in a matter of days gave her the right to stare aimlessly at wallpaper patterns on the B&Q website.

There was also the matter of Duke.

Although she'd apologised, she couldn't help feeling a little dirty for prying through his possessions like a ferret down a rabbit hole. Now she knew the owner of the dresses, and the possible reason behind Duke's hoarding, she thought it best if she steered clear.

Over the next couple of days, she sought all the supplies to make the cottage more of a home for herself. She didn't plan to rid the place of Aunty Magdalena's presence entirely. She wanted to hold on to some memory of her; just not a memory that involved plastic plants from Home Bargains.

Alice managed to find some wallpaper in the end. Nothing too gaudy, nothing William Morris expensive, just a simple floral print on a white background that she hadn't considered until the sales assistant pointed out that it would make a great feature wall alongside the duck egg blue paint she'd been admiring.

Next came the carpet. This time, she strove to avoid the sales assistants, refused to meet their gazes, murmured she was just browsing, hid behind rolls of laminate flooring, and then Marmaduke rang.

She wrestled the phone from her pocket, cursing their inadequate depth, and answered.

'You've not been around, Alice. Haven't got cold feet, have you?'

'Sorry, Duke, I've been trying to get some things sorted for the cottage.' A shop assistant advanced, moving slowly, trying to appear nonchalant, a regular jaguar on the prowl. Alice flashed her phone and a menacing glare that she usually reserved for weirdoes at bars, and he backed off. She wished she'd thought of it sooner.

'Only I thought we had a murder to investigate,' Duke said.

'After the other day, I thought it best if I make myself scarce.'

'That's all well and good, but if we're going to let every disagreement get in the way, we might as well give up now.'

'Well, that's what the police want. And what do you mean, "Every disagreement"?'

Duke chuckled down the phone. 'You've got to admit, we're both a bit hot-headed.'

Alice stopped in her tracks. '*We?*'

'You have a tendency towards aggression.'

'You sound like my Mum.'

'She's a smart woman, is Primrose.'

'I'll be there in ten minutes, Duke. You better have a brew ready. Mine's white, no sugar.'

'You're sweet enough?'

'You're catching on.'

Duke greeted her at the door with a steaming mug and a saucer of chocolate Hobnobs. She'd scoffed one before they even got to the kitchen, which was quite possibly the tidiest room in Marmaduke's house. They sat at the table, Alice helping herself to another biscuit. 'I am sorry you know, Duke?' she said.

'Forget all that. What did you and whatshisface talk about?'

'He told me about Ronnie being framed for armed robbery back in the day.'

'So, we still think this is linked to Arthur's investigation?'

'Maybe not his investigation, but I think it definitely has something to do with the Greenfields Fete.' Alice stared into her mug, mulling things over. Arthur was investigating Christopher Partridge's murder. Ronnie had been charged for an armed robbery and Christopher Partridge's murder but was ultimately cleared of both crimes. Now, they were both dead. Could the killer still be around, still worried enough about being caught that they would kill two septuagenarians?

'It's a difficult one,' said Duke. 'Arthur made a few enemies over the last few months. Any number of folk could've wanted to off him.'

'Do you think it's likely to be some little old lady whose pastry he offended?'

'You're talking about Mavis Thistlethwaite, aren't you?'

'Yes. Do you think it's likely?'

'Folk gave Arthur leeway. They understood he was grieving.'

'How long's it been?'

'Since Ethel died? Maybe nine months. They found the cancer too late. She was gone within weeks of them telling her.'

Silence again. Alice wished there was a way to summon humour to the situation, to laugh off the uncomfortable silence, but the topic was too serious. Instead, Alice looked around Duke's kitchen from her chair. The cupboards and drawers were the uniform faux-wood that's commonly found in council houses. Cheap, but passable.

The kitchen looked out onto the back garden. Here, Duke had toiled to create a masterpiece of flowers. Great blooms of purples, reds and yellows summoned bees and butterflies and, in the centre of it all, was the heart of Marmaduke's garden: his shed.

A green beast of a shed, with large windows and an apex roof.

He must have been following Alice's gaze because he said, 'That's my shed.'

'Do you know, Duke? I hadn't realised.' She smirked into her cup.

Duke had an air of pride about him. 'Do you want to see inside?'

She stared at him, blank-faced.

'It's better than it looks, trust me.'

'That's what they all say.' She stood up, rolling her eyes. 'Come on then, but I'm having the last biscuit.' She snatched it from the saucer before he had chance to protest and headed for the back door.

'It's locked.' Duke took the key from his jogging bottoms and unlocked the door.

'Why lock the door when you're the only person in the house?'

'Suppose someone broke in and got into my shed?'

'Who's going to break in?'

'You did, the other day.'

'To check if you were alive. Not to steal gardening tools.'

'Who said anything about gardening tools?'

'Where else would you keep them?'

'The airing cupboard.'

Alice had nothing to say to that. She took a bite of her biscuit and followed Duke out into the garden. She inhaled the sweet and musky aromas permeating throughout, wishing she could identify the various flowers and shrubs that made up Duke's garden. 'I have a few questions before we go in.'

Marmaduke thought it over. Alice could see that he'd got some questions of his own, the concern on his face as easy to read as *Each Peach, Pear Plum*.

'First,' Alice said, 'why is your front garden such a mess if this is the sort of thing you can achieve?'

'That's an easy one. Doug Grey's missus came round here wanting me to let folk come and traipse all over the place. I told her, I said, "My garden is for my use only, not just any old Tom, Dick or Harry with no horticultural expertise."'

'All right, so Violet Grey offers you the chance to share this with other people, and you decline? That doesn't explain the awful front garden.'

'She wouldn't stop, kept at it like a bleeding Yorkshire terrier. I thought, I'll stop the WI pestering me again. Your Aunty Magdalena had just given me the caretaking job, so I moved everything over there.'

'What about the scrap?'

'I know Tommy from the scrapyard, told him the situation, and he brought a few bits down one evening. I've had to run off a few rag and bone men, I can tell you.' Marmaduke smiled at the memory, as proud as a schnauzer.

'But why?'

'I didn't do all this work for other people, Alice. I enjoy gardening. I don't need the approval of a few old biddies to know I'm good at it.' He unlocked his shed.

'I have more questions, Duke.'

He sighed. 'Go on then.'

'Were you on the force when Christopher Partridge was killed?'

Marmaduke nodded. His jowls seemed to sink, giving him the look of a disenchanted bulldog. 'I was one of the lucky ones who got time off to enjoy the fete. Before you ask, no I didn't see a thing. None of us did. You have to understand that the Greenfields Fete was one of the biggest events in the Partridge Mews calendar. It goes back generations, and the old lord went out of his way to make sure everyone enjoyed themselves this time around.'

'Giving the perfect opportunity for murder.'

He practically winced at her response. His shoulders went up, and his face contorted into a shape that a gargoyle would be proud of. 'Don't say that. It's true, but don't say it. You sound like something out of Miss Marple.'

'Miss Marple? What is it with this Miss Marple business? Jez said the same thing. Have I developed a multitude of wrinkles I didn't know about? Has something in the last few weeks given me the face of a serial knitter?' Alice glared at Duke, before catching sight of her reflection in the shed window and stepping aside. If she had somehow gained the look of Geraldine McEwan, she didn't want to know about it.

'It's nothing to do with your age. Murder is dramatic enough without stupid pronouncements like "the perfect opportunity for murder". People kill each other, Alice. More often than not, it's a spur of the moment thing. A spouse getting angry about that evening's dinner and hitting their partner over the head with a vase. They don't mean to do it.'

Marmaduke stepped over the threshold. Alice could tell he wanted to put a stop to the conversation, but she wasn't ready to let it go. 'Are you telling me that no one plans to kill? That there's not this anger bubbling beneath the surface, ultimately leading to someone figuring out how to get away with it?'

When he turned back to her, his eyes were wide

enough she could see each indiscriminate vein on the whites. She wouldn't have been surprised if he started frothing at the mouth like a rabbit cursed with myxomatosis. 'Of course, there are folk out there who plan these things, but if you go around turning everything into a big conspiracy, you'll miss the answers.'

Alice didn't reply straight away. Firstly, because she was trying to figure out a reply, and secondly, because she'd caught a glimpse of the inner sanctum of Marmaduke's shed and all words had fled her body.

If Alice thought Marmaduke had made Aunty Magdalena's house a tip, that he lived in utter squalor surrounded by filth, it was nothing compared to what she found in his shed at that moment. Everywhere she looked, there were boxes. Cardboard boxes, wooden boxes, boxes for Walker's cheese and onion crisps with a sell by date of October 1994. Yellowing paperwork sprouted from the tears and gaps in the boxes, like weeds he'd decided were more than mere dandelions. There were supermarket bags crammed with old newspapers, and Alice couldn't help but think that the dust in their creases looked thick enough to fell an asthmatic. And the must. She almost choked on the scent of must, felt it filling her lungs. Her face felt like she'd washed it with a filthy duster. She sensed it clogging her pores, wouldn't be surprised to wake up the next morning with a nose full of blackheads.

'This is different,' she said.

Duke stepped inside and puffed out his chest. 'This is where I keep all my case notes.'

'You're actually insane, aren't you?' Alice still couldn't believe it. She followed him inside and wrapped her arms around herself, wary of touching anything.

'What do you mean? I've worked a lot of cases over the years. This is where I keep my notes.' He stated all of this matter-of-factly, as though it made perfect sense to pack his shed with dozens of boxes only fit for recycling.

Alice tried to catch a peek in one of the bags without touching it, but saw nothing more than the logo of the Partridge Mews Gazette. 'You know, you're probably breaking a ton of data protection laws keeping this stuff in here.'

'Data protection laws? I'm a detective—'

'Former detective. If anyone else catches on to what you're doing here then you're likely to be arrested.'

'I'm a *former* detective who has solved many a crime since your mother was a toddler. I'm also seventy-two years old. No one's going to arrest me for keeping important documents in my shed.' Marmaduke wiped a box with his sleeve, blew in its cracks and creaked it open, unleashing a further eruption of dust. There was nothing romantic about the sunlight catching these motes of dust, nothing a hipster could use to capture the perfect photograph. This dust was an allergy-sufferer's worst nightmare, a call to arms for Dyson vacuum cleaners the world over.

Duke had called her hot-headed, though. Maybe he wanted to prove something to her. If so, she wasn't about to give him the satisfaction. Primrose would tell her to take a deep breath, but she wasn't about to do that with the chance of asphyxiating on dust such a threat. 'All right then,' she said, after a moment, 'just what did you want to show me?'

He reached into the box and pulled out more newspaper clippings. 'This is what the Gazette printed the day after Christopher Partridge's murder.'

Alice took the newspaper from him, the dust smudging on her fingertips with the merest touch. The black and white photograph showed two young women smashing cake into one another's faces, smeared make-up, broken heels, and torn dresses, both cheered on by a bunch of revellers in the background.

'I'm guessing this fight has something to do with the murder?' Alice asked, reading the article. '*Was it a case of too much elderflower wine for these two members of the Partridge Mews Women's Institute? Young Doris Copeland (22) and Edith Simpson (22) engaged in a brawl at the Greenfields Fete yesterday afternoon. Eyewitnesses report that Mrs Simpson took Mrs Copeland unawares when she flung a Victoria Sponge at her, leading to the scene photographed. It must be noted that whilst Mrs Copeland did not initiate the fight, her mother is Elizabeth Thistlethwaite, imprisoned in 1948 for alcohol-related crimes.*'

'The fight drew everyone's attention away from the manor, meaning anyone could have entered, killed Christopher, and got away before anybody noticed.'

'Are these Thistlethwaites related to Mavis Thistlethwaite?' Alice asked, trying to see any resemblance in the photo to the café owner.

'That Doris Copeland is her cousin. They may as well be sisters, the upbringing they had. When her mother was sent to prison, Doris ended up living with her aunty and uncle. They raised her as if she were their own.'

'I think I've met her before. After Aunty Magdalena fell off the swing, I had to take her to Bulge Busters.' Alice couldn't see the connection between the fight and the murder, except that they'd taken place around the same time. 'Why do you think this fight is important?'

'She and Edith were questioned at the time to see whether they were working with Christopher's killer. They weren't. They were shocked more than anything.' Marmaduke took the paper back off Alice and placed it in the box.

'But?'

'But maybe Arthur's death might have spurred them on to remember something. They might have kept something to themselves because they felt embarrassed or guilty. Someone had died – even though they didn't mean to, Doris Copeland and Edith Simpson helped a killer go free.'

'Now who's being dramatic?'

'I'm old enough, I've earned the right.'

'Are we going to go to Doris's house then? To question her and Edith? Rough them up?' Alice grinned at him.

'You know very well we're not. I want you to go to Shakespeare Avenue and speak to Doris yourself. I, meanwhile, am going to speak to Clive. See if they know anything more.'

He left the shed and Alice followed him out, her eyes alighting on a stack of boxes in the left-hand corner. They were plastic and, written in thick, black permanent marker, was one word: Joanna.

Chapter Fourteen

Shakespeare Avenue was one of those streets that Alice never wanted to live on. Each house had been built to the same specification. With perfect lawns and posh cars in the driveways, these were homes for the painfully middle-class.

The sort of people she'd always steered clear of.

She knew her own upbringing had been more privileged than others. Both her parents worked seemingly good jobs, and she'd never really struggled, but she couldn't recall ever flaunting it in somebody's face the way these people did. She'd once seen Violet Grey wrap a cardigan around her shoulders in the middle of a heatwave, just so she could flash the designer label. Never mind the threat of sunstroke; getting one up on the other women at the WI was all she cared about.

Of course, Primrose was also a member of the WI, but Alice had always hoped it was somewhat ironically – that it all came from her mother's desire to be a member of as many groups as possible, rather than a need to show that her jam-making skills were better than anyone else's. They weren't. Primrose wasn't really the sort of mother who cooked. Meaning, she couldn't cook. It wasn't for want of trying, but after she once set fire to a baked potato in the microwave, both she and her family agreed to leave the cooking up to Norman and Alice.

Despite the fact that she never wanted to visit any of the houses on Shakespeare Avenue unless for work purposes, here she was, stood outside the door of Mrs Doris Copeland, a woman who might just have been a Stepford Wife of the modern age. If her letters to the Gazette were anything to go by.

Alice had met Doris before, but she never expected to be knocking on her front door and saying, 'Excuse me, but were you at all involved in the murder of a rich heir fifty years ago?' But then, she'd never expected to be sacked, to find two dead people and to subsequently investigate their murders, which she supposed just went to show that no one ever knew what life would throw at them. One day, you have a great career and your own mug, and the next you're out on your ear and Mary Hinds has already claimed your mug as her own.

Alice approached Mrs Copeland's front door. She supposed she shouldn't be scared, but there was a definite tension in her shoulders that she couldn't shrug off. She'd always been the same around people like Mrs Copeland. They made her feel like no matter how she behaved, she was doing something wrong – that she wasn't fulfilling the social customs as required of a twenty-five year old white woman.

She took uneasy steps down the front path, feeling like her knees were nothing more than rickety scaffolding threatening to collapse at any moment. There was also the fact that she was definitely skating close to interfering with a police investigation, and despite Marmaduke's proclamations that he was too old to be arrested, *she* certainly wasn't.

It was with these thoughts rolling through her head, gathering speed, that she rang the doorbell.

She saw the shadow of someone approaching in the frosted glass of the doors. A small someone, diminutive, but that's what these people did – they made themselves small to catch you unawares when they sprung an attack.

Alice gulped, allowed herself a deep breath and composed a smile as the door opened.

'What are you doing here?' Alice asked.

'I could ask you the same question,' Mavis Thistlethwaite said, a cigarette dangling from her mouth. 'You definitely weren't invited.'

Mavis looked just as terrifying outside the café. She wore jeans and a striped Joules top, giving her the look of a casual horse rider.

'Is Mrs Copeland in?'

Mavis shook her head. 'No, that husband of hers has taken her off to Anglesey for the week.'

Alice felt as though Mavis was about to swoop down and bake her into a pie. She supposed it was just the aura that café owners gave off – that air of menace, a look that could strike fear into the hearts of alligators.

'Did they send you?' Mavis asked, inhaling a lungful of nicotine.

'Who?'

'The social. Our Doris has a bit of a criminal record now, and you're looking to see whether she's still fit to walk the streets of Partridge Mews without a probation officer present.'

'That's not why I'm here at all.'

'You'd better come in anyway, I've just made a pot

of tea.' She ground her cigarette out on the wall and flicked it over next door's fence. 'Don't tell our Doris about that neither. She pretends I don't smoke, and I pretend I get on with her husband.'

'You don't like Mr Copeland then?' Alice closed the door behind her before following Mavis down the hall.

'Let's just say we're different sorts.'

The house was pristine – everything in its place, with neutral tones on the walls and framed photographs of Doris and her family throughout the years. A regular show-home, the place smelled exactly as Alice expected: undertones of tobacco beneath Air Wick.

When Alice stepped into the kitchen, she thought her heart would stop. It was perfect, the kind of kitchen she hoped to own one day. A bright airy room, continuing the neutral tones but with flashes of yellow here and there to add colour. The granite counter tops had an air of sophistication about them, as though Nigella Lawson would arrive at any moment licking chocolate off a wooden spoon.

'It's nice, isn't it?' Mavis said.

Alice remained open-mouthed in the doorway, her eyes struggling to take everything in. 'She's a bit house-proud, isn't she?'

'It's a good quality to have. Anyway, you still haven't told me why you're here.' Mavis collected the tea tray from the counter and carried it to the table.

Alice sat down beside Mavis. 'Marmaduke Featherstone sent me to ask Mrs Copeland some questions.'

'He's investigating Arthur's death, is he?' Mavis played mother, pouring the tea into large Whittard mugs. She handed it over. 'When the police came to ask me their questions, I knew straight away he'd get involved.'

'From what I hear, he's got a history of this sort of thing.'

'Arthur and him are cut from the same cloth. Neither of them knows when to let something go.'

'We think that Arthur's investigation might have played a part in his murder.'

Mavis smacked her lips together. 'Well of course it does. What other reason did anyone have to kill him?'

'He was in the police.'

'Meaning?'

'He'll have made a lot of enemies. Criminals he put away.'

'Arthur stopped being a policeman nearly fifteen years ago. Before that, he wasn't gadding about catching murderers, on high-speed chases throughout Cheshire in his search for justice.' Mavis chuckled a breathy laugh that soon descended into a phlegmy cough.

'Either way, Duke wanted me to ask Doris about her fight with Mrs Simpson at the fete.' Alice sipped from her mug to hide from Mavis's reaction.

When she put the mug down, Mavis was waiting for her. 'Our Doris had nothing to do with that rich pillock's death. Sure, she and Edith had their little spat, but they weren't doing it to aid any killers with their murder plots. They were fighting over shoes, if you must know.'

'Why would anyone fight over shoes?'

'They'd been sniping at each other for ages. Things came to a head, Edith threw a Victoria sponge and our Doris threw a tray of vol-au-vents.' Mavis waved it off as though it was a perfectly inadequate occurrence that she had no time for.

'And they're still friends?'

'Apart from the fact that someone was murdered and the two of them ended up feeling as though their squabble had contributed to that lad's death. They've been friends since dolls' houses. They weren't about to throw all that away over one argument.'

Alice couldn't help but feel that Mavis thought her an idiot. Maybe it was because she no longer had any close friends. Sure, there were the school-friends and university acquaintances on Facebook, but she'd never really stayed in contact with anyone, hadn't really had the drive to keep in touch. She just couldn't imagine battering a best friend with a cake and continuing a relationship. Perhaps it made her fickle. Perhaps she cared a lot about cake. Either way, she didn't understand.

'Have you any idea who might have killed Christopher Partridge?'

'We all thought it was Ronnie Butterworth, thought he'd got away with it. Now he's dead as well. Funny how the detective and the possible killer both end up dead, don't you think?'

'Technically, Arthur wasn't a detective at the time, but I understand what you're getting at.' Alice slumped against the table, resting her cheek on her right hand.

'He might not have officially been a detective, but he dedicated his time to the case, accepting any jobs they'd offer him as long as they were to do with the murder. Arthur never forgave himself for what happened.' Mavis clenched the handle of her mug so tight that her fingers looked like squashed salami.

Alice noticed the tears then. She rushed to grab the towel roll off the counter and handed a bunch of the stuff over for Mavis to blot her cheeks. 'I'm sorry, Mavis. I didn't think about how this must be upsetting you.'

'You saw my last words to him, Alice, I only wanted to give him food for thought. I never expected we wouldn't get a chance to apologise to each other.' Mavis shook her head, dabbing at her eyes.

Alice pulled her chair closer and let Mavis lean against her shoulder. 'I understand feeling guilty. My Aunty Magdalena died in another country and I still question whether I could've known, could have been there. You shared more kind words with Arthur than you did bad ones, focus on those.'

Mavis sniffed. 'I know that. It would have been different if he'd just died – men are notorious for popping their clogs when you'd least expect it – but he was murdered. Someone went into his home, the place he should feel safest, and killed him.'

'We'll find his killer, Mavis, I don't doubt that.' Alice stared straight ahead, unwilling to admit her own guilty feelings, but the more she thought about Arthur, the more she worried his killer would continue to roam free.

Fifty years after the murder of Christopher Partridge, no one had found his murderer. Even with DNA and all the technological advancements since then, there was no knowing if they'd solve this crime.

Chapter Fifteen

Alice returned to the cottage that afternoon with a Waitrose carrier bag. She'd been shopping for supplies to bake a cake, a Victoria sponge inspired by Mrs Copeland's article. She also bought herself a ready meal because there was no way she'd be returning to her parents. They needed time to calm down, or to beat oned another to a pulp, or to simply have some pre-geriatric make-up sex and have done with it.

She stared at the unopened rolls of wallpaper lined up against her wall. Then she looked around Aunty Magdalena's living room.

This had been her home away from home as a child. With her grandparents sunning it up in Whitby, Aunty Magdalena had taken on many of their duties – taking Alice when her parents had to work, buying her strawberry bonbons even though Primrose warned her about her fillings – and now Alice owned the place.

'I should've charged you rent,' she said to a photograph. 'Not telling me you'd signed the place over to me, what sort of person does that?'

She shook her head and crossed over to the kitchen with her baking things. First though, she needed to locate her cup.

When Alice had been seven years old, she and Aunty Magdalena had taken a trip to Sandbach on the bus. Not the most elegant of places, but to Alice it may as well have been Manchester. The bustle of people laughing and joking with one another was enough that Alice thought everyone should take their summer holidays there. And Aunty Magdalena took her for her first afternoon tea. Alice remembered being bewildered as the waitress brought out three tiers of sandwiches, scones, petits fours and cakes, and set it in the centre of the table, alongside a china teapot, two cups and two saucers.

'Are we rich?' she asked, trying to see each separate molecule of scone.

Aunty Magdalena had laughed and shook her head. 'We've got enough money to enjoy afternoon tea every now and then, my love. Now, what do you want to try first?'

Alice enthused about everything, but most of all, she was enraptured by the pattern on her china cup and saucer. Never before had she seen something so exquisite, so intricate. She talked about it enough on the journey back that the next time she went to visit Aunty Magdalena, her own china cup and saucer were waiting for her – Royal Albert, with bright pink flowers and gold trim, it was the prettiest thing she owned. After that, all cups of tea at Aunty Magdalena's came in her cup.

Now, Alice had to find it. She started with the cupboard above the kettle. Somehow the cup had slipped her mind, didn't seem as important as it once had, but now there was almost a butterfly battering its wings against her oesophagus in her haste to find the thing. It was an ache, an ache for a connection to Aunty Magdalena that could only be found in bone china and baking. She set each mug down on the counter as she searched, but she couldn't find the cup anywhere.

Maybe she'd moved it, knowing she was leaving Marmaduke Featherstone in charge of her house and not wanting him to break something precious.

Alice searched through every cupboard, pulling out the baking tray and utensils she'd need later and setting them aside.

Nothing.

She was considering checking the bedroom when she saw it.

Her cup, the one she'd treasured as a child, sat in the window filled with soil, a withered rose crumpling in its centre.

Tears burned her eyes, a thin film over her corneas.

She wandered over to the sink and stared closer at what had been a flower.

Alice shook her head and turned away. She made it to the sofa before collapsing in a fit of sobs. Her throat ached, locking her jaw with tension as she struggled to find breath amongst the throbbing of her heart trying to escape through her mouth.

She pressed her face against a cushion, wanted to block out the memories that rose to the forefront of her mind, of arguing with Aunty Magdalena about revision versus boys, how the job in Partridge Grove would be the making of her, how when she'd announced she was moving to Madeira with her latest husband they'd had the worst fight because Alice didn't want her to go, couldn't help but see it as betrayal. Despite the fact that they'd apologised before she'd got on the plane, Alice couldn't help but know she'd soured something Aunty Magdalena had looked forward to. Now she was dead, and there was no apologising, no way of letting her know how truly sorry she felt.

'Alice?'

She heard the front door click shut and turned to look through tear-soaked hair at Jez. 'Go away.'

'I knocked but then, well, I thought you were being attacked.'

Alice stifled another sob, wiping her hair away from her eyes. 'I'm not. Please leave.'

He wasn't moving. He clasped his hands tight in front of him. 'I can't do that.'

'You're clearly not comfortable with crying women, so just get out.' Alice held a hand against her stomach, pretty sure it wasn't happy with holding back so many sobs.

'Ben told me I had to come and invite you to tea.'

'Good for Ben.'

'He said as I shouldn't have said we aren't friends, and I treated you unfairly the other day.' Jez made his way over and sat down in front of her legs. He settled his hand on her shoulder. 'I'm the only person here right now, if you want to talk.'

Alice groaned. 'I don't want to talk, Jez. I just wanted to have a cup of tea in the cup that my Aunty bought for me, but someone – possibly Duke thinking he was performing some sort of kind gesture – has planted a rose in it. I really don't need that right now because I spoke to Mavis Thistlethwaite today and I already felt guilty enough about everything without her harping on about how mean she'd been to Arthur before he died.' She took a shaky breath. 'And, when I think that I can finally have some alone time just to cry to myself – which all women do by the way, I'm not weird – you turn up on your husband's orders to offer me food because you have no concept of how to make an apology.'

Once again, Jez was lost for words. He sat, gawping at Alice like a goldfish, and said, 'Wow. That's a lot.'

'I also want to point out that this has absolutely nothing to do with Arthur's death, and everything to do with my Aunty Magdalena.' Alice turned so that she was lying flat on her back. She stared Jez dead in the eye and said, 'Grief is stupid.'

He nodded. 'It is.'

'You're just saying that because you're scared of me right now.'

'I am.' He took a tissue from his pocket and handed it over. 'It's clean, I promise.'

She wiped her eyes, blew her nose and pocketed the tissue.

They sat in silence, Jez staring straight ahead, pressing his hands together, Alice staring at the ceiling. 'Do you know,' he said, after a few minutes, 'when my Grandad died, I couldn't watch another episode of Emmerdale? He looked so much like Seth Armstrong that I'd get upset every time I saw him, thinking about what I'd missed, how I shouldn't have been so scared of dirt because then he might have loved me more.'

Alice pulled her legs towards her, keeping them on the sofa. 'I'm sure he loved you just as much, whether or not you liked dirt.'

Jez sat back. 'I know that. He never expected me to garden, or to follow in his footsteps and become a greengrocer. He died when I was nine, but I still remember running up to my room as soon as ITV news ended, just so I wouldn't have to catch a glimpse.'

'Like I said, grief is stupid.'

'It is stupid, but it's a process. There'll be days when you're feeling perfectly fine and then something so small, so insignificant can hit you, and you'll find yourself crying in the disabled toilet of a Wetherspoon's.'

'That sounds like you're speaking from experience.'

'Do you want me to clean the cup out for you?'

'Why would you do that?'

'How else are we going to have a drink if you haven't got a cup?' He smiled at her.

'I have mugs.'

'Has a mug ever made you cry?'

'Give it a few minutes and you might.' She grinned back at him, and with a laugh he went into the kitchen to wash her cup. Maybe she did have a friend in Jez, she'd just have to remember not to forget about him this time around.

A few minutes later, cup cleaned and filled with tea, he brought it over to Alice. 'So,' he said, 'did you find out anything more about our murder?'

Alice took her cup and saucer. 'What do you mean, "our murder"? It's your murder. You're the policeman, I'm a civilian.'

He brought his own drink over to the sofa and sat down. 'You know, I seem to make a lot of drinks when I come around.'

'Another perk of being a policeman. You get to look after distraught civilians.'

'You've got a point. Anyway, have you found anything?'

'You'd better not be wearing a wire, Jez, because if this is some sort of ploy to arrest me under false pretenses, I won't be happy.'

'Are you trying to get me shirtless?'

'You're a happily married man. I'm trying nothing.' She set her saucer down on the coffee table and said, 'All right. I told my Mum about Bertram and Ronnie arguing. She said as Ronnie's been going up to the Sterling farm for years, and that a lot of folk think that Ronnie and Bertram's wife were having an affair.'

Jez chuckled. 'Yeah, you're definitely going down the wrong track with that one.'

Alice considered his words, her eyes widening with realisation. 'Ronnie's gay?'

Jez nodded. 'There's every chance Ronnie was just doing some work on the farm. They do that, you know. Farmers help one another out here and there.'

'How do you know he's gay?'

'Before you start thinking I did anything with Ronnie Butterworth, I'll say you're wrong, he just happened to frequent a few of the bars around town.' Jez shrugged and supped his brew. 'I would have gone up and asked Bertram about the argument myself, but Clive says as he doesn't think it's important to the investigation.'

'How's that going, by the way?'

Jez rubbed the bridge of his nose. 'It's one of those things. At least we have the murder weapon now, thanks to you and the charity shop. I can't believe you didn't notice it was here.'

'Considering Arthur was murdered in his own home, I didn't expect to find the thing that killed him in my cottage.' Alice scratched at the back of her head and moved her feet to avoid pins and needles. 'Were there any fingerprints? Any sign who it might be?'

'None. Whoever killed Arthur knew what they were doing.'

'And what about Ronnie? It must have been someone strong to lift him up that high.'

Jez quirked an eyebrow in her direction. 'You don't think it's suicide anymore, then?'

'At first, I did. It's the whole reason I asked you, but it just seems like an easy solution, doesn't it? Fifty years ago, Ronnie is framed for murder. He gets off and disappears. Arthur begins to investigate, Ronnie kills him and then himself? It just doesn't ring true, especially considering Ronnie was the one who started the investigation in the first place.'

'Who told you that?'

'My Mum. When Ronnie Butterworth came back after his father's death, he decided to try and solve the murder himself.'

'It's just that now we know it wasn't suicide, Alice. Someone broke Ronnie's skull with the same murder weapon they used on Arthur. We believe he was killed at Arthur's house and his body moved later.'

Goosebumps broke out down Alice's arms. Two people had been murdered only a few doors down from her and she hadn't noticed; worse, she might have unknowingly helped their killer by getting Duke out of the way.

'What's more,' Jez said, 'if the DNA is anything to go by, this is also what was used to kill Christopher Partridge fifty years ago.'

'That's something, I suppose,' Alice said.

'What is?'

'You're looking for the same person. Were there any fingerprints?'

Jez shook his head. 'No, but would you expect them? Whoever our killer is, they had a good idea what they were doing.'

'Is there anything at all?'

'They managed to pull a few fibres off the weapon.

We think they're tweed.'

'Tweed? Well, that's helpful – half the population wears tweed.'

'In this heat? Who do you know who'd wear tweed at this temperature?' Jez looked at her, somewhat disappointed.

'Well, at least we know one thing.'

'What's that?'

'If we find who killed Christopher, we find who killed Arthur and Ronnie.'

'And that's about all we've got to be going on with.'

Alice nodded. She hadn't expected it would be easy finding a murderer, but she'd thought there'd be more evidence to help them. As it stood, she was looking for an OAP who enjoyed tweed and canine ornaments of an indiscriminate breed. If she could solve this, she was going to start having a jab at the Telegraph's cryptic crossword.

Chapter Sixteen

Alice didn't bother going to Jez's for tea, needing some time alone, but she thanked him all the same. She was also certain he'd broken a few laws by giving her information about the case, and whilst she wanted a friend, she didn't want to lose said friend their job – she knew full well how that felt.

Besides, she still wanted to know what Bertram and Ronnie had been arguing about. 'I'm sure Bertram mentioned the gun and the robbery,' Alice said to Duke the next morning. She called round as soon as she finished breakfast to relay the new information to him.

Duke wasn't fully awake, despite the late hour. He goggled at her and said, 'If it bothers you that much, we'll go up to the farm today. But you're buying me a bacon sandwich.'

'Is that all it takes?'

'For now, yes.'

Once again, Alice waited in the car whilst Duke got changed, and they were on their way out of Partridge Mews towards the Sterlings' farm. Many farmers were finding it wasn't enough to just be a farm anymore – they were constantly expected to take on new responsibilities to make themselves seem more worthwhile to the community. If it wasn't sheep farmers allowing all and sundry to come and see real-life lambing, it was dairy farmers allowing folk to go and milk a few cows now and then. They'd pay for the experience, and everyone agreed new life skills had been learned.

Ronnie Butterworth had his little farm shop. It had been started by his father and sold fruit and vegetables and locally produced jams from the WI.

Meanwhile, Bertram Sterling owned Hartsclough Farm. Only a stone's throw away from Brook Farm, it was renowned for its farm shop (selling locally sourced honey and food preserves) and adjacent café, all run by Bertram's wife. Everyone agreed that although she was a teapot of a woman, short, stout and completely nondescript, Flora Sterling had a flare for management rivalled only by Mavis Thistlethwaite. She'd turned the place around in recent years, flipping an old barn into an eatery that hipsters zoned in on.

They parked. Duke took one look at the house and went inside the café. Alice rolled her eyes and followed him.

A few diners chatted happily away in the café area, which Duke fast approached, seating himself next to one of the windows. Flora had taken full advantage of the view by having many of the walls replaced with glass, so her patrons could see out across the fields towards the tors. There was a homely scent about the place – that of freshly-baked bread and bacon, just what Duke had asked of Alice.

She went to sit with him and waited to be served.

'You know, we could have gone straight up to the house and spoke to Bertram,' she said, glancing at the menu. Fact was, she worried Mavis would find out that one of the Valentines had eaten at a different café to her own and would start another campaign in the Gazette.

'Feel free,' Duke said. 'You go knock on his door right now and say, "I heard you arguing about a fifty-year-old murder, and now your friend and brother are dead, can I ask you a few questions?" See if it works.'

Alice swallowed hard. 'I see what you mean.'

'Good, because it took you so long to get here that I now fancy a full English. Do you think you can stretch to that?' Not that it mattered; the waiter arrived and within moments, Duke had ordered two full Englishes and a pot of tea.

'I don't have a job you know, Duke, and I already had breakfast.'

'Do you want me to call him back and cancel the order?'

'I never said anything about that.'

'Don't worry about things so much, Alice. We'll speak to Bertram and find out just what it was that he and Ronnie were talking about.'

They didn't have to wait long. Flora Sterling came out of the kitchen, carrying a plastic tray and with a look of fury on her face. She slammed the tray down on the table next to them, her glower firmly fixed. 'Marmaduke Featherstone!' she exclaimed, her voice packed with gravel. 'What in the good Lord's name are you doing in my restaurant when one of your oldest friends is sitting next door grieving?'

Alice averted her eyes.

'Don't you look like that, lovely. I know what your game is. Or do you think I'd forget the closest thing Magdalena Valentine had to a daughter?'

Other customers were looking now, not sure whether to laugh or hide.

'Flo–'

'There's no use being like that, Duke. Both of you get your backsides over to my house now, and I'll fetch your food in a minute.' Flora spun on her heel and stormed back to the kitchen, leaving Alice speechless.

Duke, meanwhile, had a grin on his face. 'I love it when she gets angry.'

Alice looked from Duke to the kitchen and back again. 'Are you saying you planned this?'

'It's like I said, Alice. We can't go up and start asking questions, but if we're sent, that's a different matter entirely.' Duke stood up.

'You're saying we couldn't just turn up and offer our condolences?' Alice followed him out the door.

'We could, but where's the fun in that?'

They turned left and headed towards the front door of the house. Bertram stood there, looking ashen, his cheeks pale and hollow. He reminded Alice somewhat of a melon with its insides scooped out. He just looked empty.

She understood how he was feeling. There's just no making sense of the world when you're recalibrating to the loss of someone close. Bertram's brother was dead. No matter how much she wanted to help solve the case, she had to remember his feelings as well. Something she hadn't considered before.

Duke shook Bertram's hand and offered a sympathetic smile. 'Your missus says as we're to come up to the big house for our breakfast.'

Bertram nodded his head. 'That's what I heard, too.'

'I don't know what to say, Mr Sterling. I'm sorry,' Alice said.

'I appreciate the honesty. Aren't you the girl who–'

'She found Arthur's body, yes.' Duke nodded and stepped past Bertram into the house. 'Come on you two, I'm starving.'

'I was going to say, who bought the mop bucket.'

Alice nodded as they watched Duke scoot down the hall. 'He's got a way with words, hasn't he?' She shook Bertram's hand. 'My name's Alice Valentine. If you read the papers then I recently contributed to the deaths of three OAPs. I shouldn't worry.'

Bertram looked more stricken than he had done previously and said, 'The kitchen's just through there.'

'Good to know.' She nodded and followed the path Duke had taken, stopped only by the coat hooks on the wall, from which hung two tweed jackets – his and hers – and a tweed flat cap. Alice hadn't considered that Arthur's own brother could have something to do with his death, and farmers did have a propensity for wearing tweed. Perhaps it was an unfortunate coincidence that his clothes were made from the same fibres found on the weapon used to kill his brother. Sure, she felt sorry for Bertram, but that meant understanding his grief, not avoiding the fact he could be a murderer.

They were met in the farm's kitchen by Flora. She'd walked down a ginnel that connected the house and the café's kitchen to bring them their food. 'Now, I expect you to cheer up that husband of mine,' she said, placing their plates on the table. 'And, as always, Duke, these are free of charge.'

She walked back down the steps towards the café, leaving the three of them to their own devices.

'What does she mean, as always?' Alice asked.

'That's a tale for another day.' Duke quickly tucked

into his food, packing his mouth with bacon and tomatoes. He sloshed them around as though his tongue was a washing machine.

Bertram joined them at the table, a lone mug of tea sat in front of him. 'You heard us arguing,' he said, directing his words towards Alice.

Startled, she spoke as she chewed her toast. 'I did, but I didn't really hear what you said.' She thought it best to lie. The fact was, she remembered most everything Bertram and Ronnie had discussed. It had only been a few short sentences, but she spent nights running their every word through her mind, repeatedly, trying to figure out if they'd said something incriminating, something that would get her closer to finding a killer.

Bertram's shoulders slumped. He hunched forward and stared down into his mug. 'Oh. Only, I hoped you might be able to shed some light.'

'I'm not a detective anymore,' Duke said, slurping his tea. He creased his neck against something he'd swallowed the wrong way. 'You really should speak to Clive.'

Bertram's eyes widened, bewilderment etched into every wrinkle on his face. 'Clive? I can't speak to Clive. That'd be making it official. No, you might be retired but you're still dipping your toe in every now and then, aren't you?'

Alice sighed and glanced at Duke. 'He's right, you know.'

'I suppose we'll just have to tell him, Alice.'

'It's supposed to be an interrogation, not an assertion.'

'Then interrogate the man. Get your answers.'

Bertram looked more confused than a young man

faced with his first papaya. 'Have you two gone completely off your rockers?'

Alice tore a chunk off her toast and dipped it into the yolk of her egg. 'The truth is that we came up here today to ask you just what you and Ronnie were arguing about when I came to buy that mop bucket.'

'How is it, by the way?'

'How's what?'

'The mop bucket.'

Alice ate the bite of toast. 'I haven't had chance to use it yet.'

'Don't avoid the conversation, Bertie. This doesn't have to go any further than this kitchen. We all understand how you must be feeling.'

'My brother is dead, Duke. I don't really care about my dispute with Ronnie. I just want someone to find out who killed him.' Bertram stood up and crossed the room to stare out the window. 'I accused Ronnie of sheep rustling.'

Alice shook her head. 'That doesn't make any sense. I heard you mention a gun and the robbery.'

He turned back to face her. 'You heard a few lines of an argument. Ronnie said if I was so sure he'd stolen my sheep, I should go to the police. I said I couldn't because he'd already got a history.'

'He got off. How is that a history?'

'He might have done, but there are folk in town who still blame him. Mud sticks.'

'All right then, Bertie, where did these sheep disappear from?' Duke asked.

He thought for a moment. 'Down the bottom field, the one with the gate onto the road.'

Alice would have said more but Duke interrupted, saying, 'Your food's getting cold, Alice. Eat up.'

She looked down at Duke's plate. 'You've finished?'

'I told you I was hungry. Now go on, Flora's food is best at its hottest.'

Bertram headed towards the kitchen door. 'I'm going for a lie down. I hope you understand. You can let yourself out, Duke?'

He didn't give them a chance to reply before he disappeared down the hall. They listened to his footsteps as he creaked his way up the stairs. Moments later, they heard the awful sound of an older man sobbing.

Alice could only imagine the way his body would be wracked with grief, buckling beneath its pressure. 'He's not telling the whole truth,' she said.

Duke nodded. 'Course he isn't. He's recalled a story there, not a memory. He knew we'd be coming.'

'What do we do?' she asked.

'What have we been doing all along?'

Alice gave him a questioning look as she swallowed a chunk of hash brown.

'Investigating, Alice. We keep investigating.'

Chapter Seventeen

'It just doesn't make sense that she'd give you all your meals on the house,' Alice said.

They'd pulled to the side of the road so Duke could look at the field where Bertram claimed he'd lost his sheep, a regular Little Bo Peep.

'I told you, that's a tale for another day,' Duke replied. He examined the fence closely, getting up close and personal with the wire, running his fingers along it.

'I don't know why you're bothering. We both know that Bertram is lying about the sheep rustling.' She leaned against the bonnet of the car; her arms folded.

'We have to check.'

'I don't see that there's any need to be thorough. Bertram wants us to solve his brother's murder. Let's just go back to yours and go through your paperwork again. We know that the same person who killed Arthur and Ronnie killed Christopher.'

'You make a lot of assumptions, don't you?'

'It's the same murder weapon.'

He straightened and turned to face her, holding a branch away from his face to get a proper look. 'Just because it's the same murder weapon, it doesn't mean it's the same culprit. Someone could have found the ornament and decided to kill Arthur with it for some sort of symmetry.' He sighed and made his way back through the tall grass. 'You're not wrong, though. This would be the clear path for rustlers to take some sheep. No one's been through here in a long while.'

Alice clapped her hands together. 'Thank you. Now get in the car.'

Duke got into the passenger seat. 'I had to check, Alice.'

'You didn't. You could've just listened to Alice, but no, you had me drive down here for some proof that the sheep we knew hadn't been stolen had been stolen.' She shook her head as they pulled back onto the road. 'And what did we find out, Duke?'

'You're enjoying this.'

'We found out the sheep hadn't been stolen. What a complete waste of time this has been, time that could've been spent in your shed.'

'You don't like my shed.'

'I don't like your shed, but your shed is where all of the top-secret evidence is.'

'Flora's food has made you really bolshie, hasn't it?'

'That and a conversation I had with Jez last night.'

Duke groaned.

'What? That had better be indigestion, you didn't seriously just groan.' Alice kept her eyes on the road, flabbergasted at Duke's response. 'I'm allowed friends.'

'I don't dispute that, but making friends with a detective? Surely there are more interesting people around.'

'You were a detective.'

'Yes, so you know I'm speaking from experience.'

Alice rolled her eyes. She felt as though she

understood criminals now. With Duke's personality if he had been the detective in charge, she'd have committed crimes just to spite him.

Chapter Eighteen

They returned to Duke's shed so Alice could go through his box of evidence related to the Christopher Partridge case. She eyed the photograph of Mrs Copeland and her friend Edith going at it like a pair of rabid walruses. Maybe the world of the WI really was a cut-throat business. She'd heard stories from her mother, but she'd always believed them to be a farce, concocted to explain the reasons behind a lost jam competition. Apparently, the secretary didn't believe chilli was a truly British jam flavour. She'd said that the shock on the palate was really more suited to savoury meals and that it hadn't been a suitable accompaniment to clotted cream.

Alice read some paperwork related to Christopher's murder. Sergeant Creswell Constable had been the man in charge back in the day. He'd been the one to leave Arthur in charge of guarding Greenfields, whilst he and the rest of the men went to investigate the possible armed robbery.

'This is the first time I've seen it referred to as only a *possible* armed robbery,' Alice said, taking the papers out to Duke. He'd chosen to laze about in a sun lounger, napping and occasionally reading the *Radio Times*.

He looked as though he was going to try sitting up, but then he fell back against the lounger. 'Of course, Sergeant Constable said it was only a possible armed robbery. There'd been no armed robbery, had there? He'd look a great pillock, going around telling everyone there'd been an armed robbery when nothing had been nicked and the gun was found stashed behind the counter.'

Alice nodded, feeling suitably chastised. 'Are you saying the police changed their story, then?'

'They didn't change their story, Alice. When they left Greenfields, they believed they were headed towards an armed robbery at a jewellers. They didn't know it had been a ploy to get them away so someone could go in and nobble the heir.'

'I don't suppose they know who reported the robbery, do they?'

He shook his head. 'Apparently they have no idea. The person who took the call said they heard a huge row in the background, and that was enough for them to take the caller seriously.'

'I mean, they were being told about an armed robbery. I think you'd be pretty concerned even without a row.'

'You could be right.' Duke settled himself down in his lounger, his eyes closed. 'Is that all? Only I was having quite the daydream about Rula Lenska.'

Alice rolled her eyes and returned to the shed. She stopped at the door and asked, 'What did Arthur have to say about it all?'

Duke opened his right eye. 'What do you mean?'

'After he recovered from his attack, what did he have to say?'

'He didn't see his attacker. Luckily, he'd been wearing his hat when they hit him. Otherwise, it might have been curtains for him as well.'

'They got him in the end though, didn't they?' Alice leaned against the door jamb of the shed, holding the papers close to her chest. 'I just don't understand any of this, Duke. What motive did anyone have to kill Christopher?'

'You're joking, aren't you? He was the heir of Greenfields. That place has been a source of controversy for centuries. A bunch of toffee-nosed prigs sitting in the big house, looking down on all of us. The bleeding town is named after the family, for crying out loud.'

'I thought it was just a happy coincidence,' she said, unable to meet his gaze.

'I wouldn't call it happy.' Duke's cheeks were red, indignation blooming across his face like poppies. 'The fact of the matter is, Alice, that you see Christopher Partridge as a victim. But he was a selfish, yellow-bellied terror who looked at folk as though they were vermin. There were a great number of people that wanted to see him dead, so no one particularly minded when someone offed him.'

'I didn't even know he existed until a few weeks ago.'

'I'm not having a go at you.' He really did sit up now, shielding his eyes from the sun so he could look at her directly. 'I remember when we first started looking into his murder. We searched Greenfields, Partridge Mews, everywhere we could think of, looking for scraps of evidence. We looked into the old lord's finances. Clutching at straws, we were. But whenever you asked folk if they knew anything about Christopher's death, they all said a variation on the same thing: "I don't know who did it, but I'd like to buy them a drink."'

'I don't know what to say. I thought we were looking for a real bad guy, the lowest of the low, moustache-twirling and all that. I never expected they'd been doing everyone a favour.'

'Don't get me wrong, murder is still an awful crime. Christopher was only about your age. There's every chance he could've grown up and mended his ways, but we'll never know.'

'Meaning his legacy is a bad one.' Alice shook her head. 'We're not doing this to help Christopher though, are we?'

Duke offered her a smile. 'No, we're not. We're doing this for Arthur.'

'So no matter how vile a person Christopher was, he doesn't matter.'

'I like the sound of that.'

When Alice returned to Duke's paperwork, she found out just what a horrible person Christopher could be. First, there were the accounts from his workers. His groundskeeper had once threatened to knock his block off when Christopher had ridden his horse through the south fields, ruining the crop. There'd been some dispute about Christopher's behaviour at the mayor's Yuletide Pageant, which involved drink, debauchery and the possible pregnancy and subsequent dismissal of a certain Isobel Ramsbottom. A cyclist broke his arm after Christopher stole a tractor, mowed him down, passed out at the wheel and knocked down a drystone wall, releasing a flock of sheep into the road which then made its way into Partridge Mews and made a mess of a war monument. He remained completely unaware until he awoke in hospital, hungover. His father claimed Christopher suffered from an undiagnosed mental illness and sent him off to Rhyl for a few months.

Christopher returned with a wife in tow. Clementine, Christopher's cousin, had originally been sent with him as a nurse and supposed companion to keep him out of mischief. The Welsh air worked its magic on the two of them and they married – a shotgun wedding by anyone's standards.

Alice read more of Duke's notes. She now recognised the wiry scrawl as his own handwriting as he'd documented everything he'd been told or remembered.

Clementine's presence in Christopher's life calmed him somewhat. No more did he get into drunken brawls. He was still an arrogant prig, but he kept himself away from the town, only venturing as far as the farms nearest Greenfields.

His father, inspired by the change, chose to give Christopher more responsibilities. They were due to make a grand announcement at the Greenfields Fete, but they'd had the opportunity taken away from them.

Clementine inherited Christopher's estate and, when the old lord died, Greenfields.

'Did Clementine kill her husband?' Alice stepped outside and sat down with her back against the shed. She shaded her eyes with her hands as she spoke to Duke.

Duke, meanwhile, had discovered a pair of oversized black sunglasses, so she had to simply hope he was awake. He made some sort of gruff noise in the back of his throat and said, 'Clementine didn't kill him. I happen to know she was otherwise engaged.'

'You believe her alibi, then?'

'I *am* her alibi. Clem and I go way back. She found out I'd been given time off to enjoy the fete and asked if I wanted to see the grounds.' He grinned, the sun illuminating each and every bit of yellow in his teeth.

Alice found herself smiling back. 'Are you telling me you were getting up to extra-marital business with Clementine Partridge?'

'I'm telling you nothing. Your dirty mind's painting pictures you want to see. What else have you found?'

What Alice found was an uncomfortable question lurking at the back of her mind. Despite the lurch in her stomach at the thought of such things, she asked, 'Just how much do you know about this case, Duke?'

He sat up, although it took time. Regardless of age, sun loungers are notoriously difficult to get out of. 'Are you asking me if I killed Christopher?'

She quickly shook her head. 'That's not what I meant. I just wondered what you know.'

'Everything I know is in that shed. I suggest you look at it before accusing folk.' He'd lifted his sunglasses to reveal eyes like shrivelled beetles squinting at her.

'I wasn't accusing you. The timeline is iffy, Duke. Clementine Partridge married her cousin, who popped his clogs soon after, leaving her a ton of money. Are you sure she didn't have a policeman take her out to provide her with a strong alibi?'

Duke sighed. 'Of course, I thought that back in the day. We had a great many arguments. Fact is, I stopped talking to her, thought it best to keep things professional just in case she'd had her husband bludgeoned. Nobody else knows what we got up to that day because she gave Ronnie an alibi.'

'How does that work?'

'It worked out best for everyone. No one found out about me and her, and the charges against Ronnie were dropped.'

'You're seriously telling me that a dead man's wife gave his possible murderer an alibi and the police didn't think there was a chance she knew who did it.'

'You're casting aspersions now, Alice. Tread careful, you can offend a great many folk by accusing them of murder.'

'We're going to have to go and see Clementine, Duke.'

'I thought we might.'

Chapter Nineteen

Greenfields Hall was a sandstone manor on the edge of Partridge Mews. Alice recalled going there on a school trip. It must have been in year five because she knew she'd been jealous of the year twos getting to go to Beeston Castle while she was stuck traipsing around a stately home. Her teachers called it a cultural highlight for the children of Partridge Mews; her classmates called it a giant sandcastle. They were nine and ten-year-olds. Unless they were future architects, they weren't going to care about the recent refit of the foyer to include new toilets. They weren't even allowed to use the toilet. She soon realised the school had only been invited in the hopes the children would spend extortionate amounts in the gift shop.

When Alice told this story to Duke, he chuckled and said, 'Yeah, Clementine has always had a head for business. You've got to, nowadays. Even if you're born into money, you have to know how to keep it.'

'I'm guessing you're speaking from experience?'

'That's a story for another day, Alice. If you don't mind, I'm going to have a nap. Wake me up when we get there.'

They only had a few minutes to go until she'd be pulling up in the car park, but Alice didn't say anything. If Duke wanted to give off the aloof impression that he wasn't bothered by his wealth, or lack thereof, then she'd let him. She certainly wasn't going to ask a man who supposedly came from old money why he lived in a house that could have been Stig of the Dump's retirement home.

An assortment of vans, lorries and skips surrounded them, looking more like they'd parked in a scrapyard than outside Partridge Mews's answer to Downton Abbey.

Alice flashed a questioning glance towards Duke, but he still feigned slumber. With a well-placed whack to the arm, he soon woke up.

'What did you do that for?'

'You spend too much time dozing. I've thought you were dead once already, I didn't want to make the same mistake.' She winked at him and pointed out the vehicles. 'What do you think they're doing here?'

He yawned, stretching his arms out above his head to reveal the thick, curly hairs on his stomach. 'That'll be a question for Clementine. I can imagine it's just the sort of thing that's going to help us to solve this murder, asking her what a load of old trucks are doing in her car park.'

'Have you always been this sarcastic or did it come in a box set with filth and untidiness?'

'Better than that. I took an evening class.'

Alice hid a smirk by getting out of the car.

She had to admit that the building was impressive. Now she was older, she understood just what her teachers were getting at all those years before, apart from the fact that half of the building had been hidden behind a ton of scaffolding and sheets, giving it the look of an architectural Frankenstein.

The more recent addition of a car park meant that people had to walk down the original drive, highlighting the effort spent on the gardens.

'You must be in your element here,' she said to Duke, stopping to admire topiary in the shape of a swan.

He shrugged. 'I like gardens. This is more a park than anything.'

'Impressive, though, isn't it?'

'Aye, I'll give you that. It's definitely impressive.'

They continued their walk up the old path, Alice stopping every now and then to look more closely at the flower beds. Clearly, there was something to be said about the gardeners of Partridge Mews. In recent weeks, she'd seen the care people put into their gardens, and whilst she knew this couldn't all be Clementine's work – there was simply too much ground for one person to manage – she found it astounding that so many people would spend their free time on what she'd always seen as a trivial pursuit.

'It's all for the bleeding garden safari, you know?' Duke said, a rough edge to his voice which Alice had come to associate with judgement.

'Can't Clementine just enjoy the sight of a beautiful lawn?'

'I know Clem, she'd be much happier if this place were overrun with wildflowers and weeds.'

'He's right, I'm afraid.'

Alice's shock at Duke's answer was nothing compared to when she realised they were being watched. An older woman lazed against the trunk of an old tree, looking as relaxed as a sunbathing cat. It appeared they'd interrupted her reading.

A large, droopy sunhat shaded her face, despite the sun, and her clothes were over-sized as well, in neutral tones of brown and cream with splashes of orange and teal in the many bangles she wore and the thin silk scarf around her throat. Clementine Partridge was the epitome of an ageing bohemian, the classic Glastonbury dweller, another in a long line of eccentrics.

Alice chose to focus on the book. 'What're you reading?'

Clementine looked down at the thick tome, almost surprised to see it in her lap. 'Oh, this?' She flashed them the cover. '*A Game of Thrones.* I've read it a few times already, but my grandson recently got into the television show and he insists I read it again with him. He'll give up by page fifty. He hasn't got a lot of time on his hands, what with being the premier queer poet of Tunbridge Wells.'

Alice didn't know what to say. She opened and closed her mouth a few times, becoming very aware that she looked like an anthropomorphic goldfish that Duke had chosen to take on a day out.

'Aren't you going to introduce me, Duke? The poor girl looks fit to collapse due to sheer embarrassment.'

Despite Clementine's words, Duke grinned from ear to ear. 'Nice to see you too, Clem.'

Clementine tilted her sunhat back and met Alice's gaze. This only made things worse. She had an almost regal air about her. Her make-up looked as though it had been professionally done. She'd gone with orange and teal around the eyes as well, with a nude lipstick, and it turned out that a woman is never too old for highlighter because Clementine's looked fit to bring down a satellite. 'I'm Clementine,' she said, 'and Duke was quite right in saying that I'd prefer the place overgrown with weeds. I can't bear the idea of taming the earth, but I hired a new manager and she insists we bring Greenfields into the modern day.'

She stood up with all the elasticity of a Staffordshire gymnast and shook Alice's hand.

'I'm Alice,' she said, still feeling bewildered by the entire situation, 'I lost my job after sending a ninety-three-year-old woman to a Zumba class, and now I'm helping Duke to investigate a murder.'

Clementine offered Alice a smile. 'Well, that simply sounds like ageism to me. Why shouldn't a ninety-three-year-old woman enjoy the benefits of Zumba? I don't know about this murder business, so we may as well go inside for a cappuccino.'

With that, she took Alice by the arm and led her towards the manor, pointing out all the recent changes that her new team of gardeners had made. 'And right here, there used to be a lovely patch of ragwort. I've spent many a long day watching seasonal insects flit around here, and now it's gone to be replaced with more appropriate flowers as befit a modern wedding venue.'

'You're finally allowing the redevelopment, then?' Duke asked.

Clementine nodded. 'I simply cannot afford the upkeep of the place without doing so. It worked perfectly when I had money coming in from the university, but you know full well I've never been able to save, so I'm coming out of retirement to host weddings from across the country. I ought to tell them that marriage is a medieval practice that should have gone out with blancmange, but Ingrid says I'll soon lose business.'

'It would be a bit like a pastry chef warning of diabetes,' Alice said.

'I know. I'm told I'll never have to see the ceremonies, which is a blessing.'

They climbed the front steps and entered the house. The foyer was something out of a film, with its checkerboard floor and grand staircase branching off into two separate wings of the house. A coffin-sized crystal chandelier dangled overhead, reflecting like diamond shards on the wood-slatted walls.

Clementine led them past the staircase, down the hall, and into the living room. Worlds apart from the foyer, this was a homely space with its red three-piece suite, thick cushions, family photographs and old-fashioned wallpaper that made it feel like stepping into someone's grandmother's house. Except for the feeling that it was all very expensive and that the flat-screen television in the corner probably cost more than three months' rent.

'Go on, sit,' Clementine insisted. 'I'll just go through to the kitchens and see what I can find.'

Duke plopped himself onto the sofa, nestling his backside in as though trying to properly acquaint the cushion with his buttocks. 'Ah, that's nice, that is. You can tell that's quality.'

Alice sat in the armchair. She immediately understood what Duke was talking about.

'This is the type of cushion I want my coffin lined with.'

'Shall we ring the undertakers now and ask them to reserve some stock?'

'It couldn't hurt.' He closed his eyes and leant his head back against the sofa, basking in its comfort. Duke really did remind Alice of a cat; his tendency to doze, his love of good cushions. If he revealed his great-grandfather was a feline, she wouldn't have been surprised.

Clementine returned, took one look at Duke and laughed. 'He never changes.'

She'd taken off her hat before returning, revealing thick brown hair backcombed into something reminiscent of a beehive, the rest left to settle in curls down her back. Alice couldn't believe the confidence she exuded; it practically eked out of Clementine's pores.

'I asked one of the girls to bring our drinks through. There may be cakes. I'm not really sure what goes on down there.'

'Still avoiding shopping?' Duke asked, opening his right eye.

'I simply cannot bring myself to waste time dawdling through a supermarket. It's tedious. All that waiting, and the trolley pushing, and the endless dithering. No, I'm more than happy for Cyrus to take care of all that.'

'Cyrus?' Alice asked.

'My grandson. We chat to one another via Skype most days. He's usually asking my opinion on some verse of his – I keep telling him not to shy away from being provocative, but that's a story for another day. I believe you wanted to chat to me about murder?'

There was a breathy drawl to Clementine's speech which Alice thought must come from her tendency to talk as fast as humanly possible. She'd always anticipated that those of a higher class would enunciate their words, speaking slowly so as to drain each syllable from a word, but Clementine spoke greedily, as if there was a chance the words would dry up.

'You don't hold back, do you?' Alice ran her tongue

along her teeth, her mouth as dry as Blackpool beach in a heatwave.

Clementine smiled, a mere parting of the lips, a glimmer in her eyes. 'There's no point beating about the bush with pleasantries. Politeness never got me anywhere, did it, Duke?'

Both his eyes shot open at this. He scrambled to sit up straight. Clearly, he'd been more tired than Alice thought. 'I'm not quite sure what you're talking about there.'

Clementine looked set to tell Alice herself when there was a knock at the door and a slim girl entered the room carrying a plastic tray. She brought over their drinks, cappuccinos as requested, and some slivers of cakes on another china saucer. 'Thank you, Tracey. Everything looks perfect.'

They watched her leave before Clementine said, 'She's one of the assistants Ingrid brought in for the revamp. Apparently, she's going to open one of the drawing rooms in that wing as some sort of café. Not that there's any real need for another eatery in Partridge Mews, but I suppose she wishes to bring in a more higher-class of customer than, say, Thistlethwaite's.'

'I like Thistlethwaite's,' Alice said.

'As do I. You should listen to my words before responding, as nobody likes to look the fool.' Clementine folded her arms. 'Either way, these cakes are part of a test menu they've concocted. I can't say I've tried them.'

'Alice makes cakes. Good ones, if her mother's words are anything to go by.'

She stared at Duke, open-mouthed. 'When did she tell you about my baking?'

'She rang me up after you found Arthur's body. Said

that if I came to the cottage one day and found you surrounded by baking trays, you'd be feeling the weight of the world, so I should go easy on you and save her a slice of chocolate cake.' He winked and helped himself to something small, square and blue.

Alice shook her head and turned back to Clementine. 'If the new development is going to put money in your pocket, it can't be too bad, can it?'

'I know that it's necessary. And they're building it in the west wing, so it doesn't affect me too much. We haven't used it since the war.'

'I didn't know anywhere in Cheshire was bombed.' Alice said. She'd just sampled the corner of the chocolate cake to find it as dry as sandpaper, but the cappuccino was still too hot for her to drink.

Clementine had no issues with her drink, slurping it and steaming at the mouth like a new age dragon. 'No, we weren't bombed. My uncle and his wife housed some soldiers who required rehabilitation and put them up in the west wing. There were a few who didn't recover and so, being a superstitious fellow, he wouldn't allow any of us to use it.'

Alice and Duke shared a conspiratorial look with one another. It was seen by a perceptive Clementine, who asked, 'What did that look mean?'

'The thing is, Clem,' Duke said, placing his hand on her wrist, 'Arthur Sterling and Ronnie Butterworth have both been murdered.'

A tremor ran through Clementine's body. She hissed through her teeth and bowed her head. 'I thought something like this would happen. I imagine the look you just shared had something to do with it.'

'The murder weapon was the same as the one used to kill Christopher back in 1965. Some sort of dog ornament. The police can't really tell much more beyond it being canine in appearance.'

Clementine nodded. 'And you think it was hidden here but with all the redevelopments going on, the killer got scared and came to collect it?'

'When did you get so perceptive?' Alice asked. She chanced a sip of her drink and caught only foam in her gullet.

'I stated a fact and you gave Duke a glance you perhaps thought was secretive but which looked more theatrical than Brian Blessed in drag. You were superbly easy to read.' Clementine stopped to pick up a slice of something pink and spongey. She took one bite before daintily setting the remainder of the cake down and rubbing the crumbs between her fingers, dissatisfied.

'It's a possibility though, isn't it, Duke?' Alice asked, desperately searching for support.

'Have you used that part of the house at all since then?' he asked.

Clementine wound a strand of hair around her finger as she spoke, as though the mere movement was enough to unlock her memories. Perhaps it was. When Alice looked at Clementine, she couldn't help questioning if she'd been an understudy for Samantha in Bewitched. 'No,' she said, eventually. 'I suppose superstition really did affect us all. Bearing in mind that my uncle didn't die until the nineteen-eighties and by then I was living in West Berlin with Wilson.'

'I thought you lived here the entire time,' Alice said.

'I had to have a life, Alice. You must understand that. I stayed here for a few years after Christopher died, learning how to manage the estate, but eventually I found my drive for education again, and after some careful talks I left.'

'Education makes you sound young. How old were you when you married Christopher?'

'I must've been sixteen or seventeen. Originally, I thought I was just going to chaperone a mentally unstable relative. I never envisaged a grand holiday in Wales from our family.' The recollection brought a smile to Clementine's face. 'With my father's blessing, we married and came back. It made my uncle happy, in any case.'

'He wanted Christopher to marry you?'

'He wanted Christopher to calm down.'

'Did he?'

She nodded. 'He did, but that was nothing to do with me. That was all down to Ronnie.'

'Our Ronnie? Ronnie Butterworth?' Alice gently set her cappuccino down on the table, worried she'd spill it on a section of expensive carpet.

'Let's skip straight to the big revelation, shall we? I was the greatest beard in Partridge Mews. Christopher and Ronnie were in a relationship. It was a regular lord and groundskeeper deal. Like *Lady Chatterley's Lover,* only they're both men and there were fewer girdles.'

Alice shook her head and leaned back against the chair. 'But why did you stay with him?' She caught a warning glance from Duke, but it was too late.

'They were together before Christopher was sent to Wales. He told me the situation after a couple of weeks. I'd grown tired of the constant coastal walks. I knew he was of sound mind, so I came out and asked him just what his father was thinking.'

Alice felt a simmering anger rise in her chest at the injustice she knew had been made towards Christopher. His bad behaviour made sense to her. 'His father didn't like the fact that Christopher was gay?'

'Christopher was sent to Wales because his father claimed he suffered from mental health issues that could only be cured by fresh air. I came up with a plan that meant he could keep seeing Ronnie and I could get out from under my parent's feet and earn some money in the process.'

'It was a marriage of convenience,' Duke uttered.

'Is that why you gave Ronnie the alibi?'

'I knew he would never harm a single hair on Christopher's head. Theirs was the purest love I ever witnessed, until somebody ended it for them.' She screwed her eyes shut and leaned forward, allowing herself a few deep breaths before sitting back up, composed, as though it had never happened.

'Did the police know about their relationship?'

'My father was the sergeant at the time. He knew about the two of them, but he kept it quiet.'

'But what about now? Do the police know?'

'I'm assured they'll keep it out of any reports unless absolutely necessary. My brother is the inspector in charge of the case.'

Alice glanced at Duke. 'Do I know him?'

'I should think so,' Duke said. 'Clive Constable is Clementine's brother. I thought you knew.'

'Yes, Clive is my brother. Yes, he's protecting familial secrets because both he and I know the way local gossip can affect a person. No, he doesn't believe it has any bearing on the reason why Christopher was killed. I'm sure that, had he been old enough, Clive would have been in Arthur's place.' She downed the rest of her drink before slamming it on the edge of the table.

Alice couldn't quite understand Clementine's frenetic energy. When they'd arrived, she gave off an aloof impression, as though she knew life was a rollercoaster and she was simply along to enjoy the ride. Yet the memories of fifty years ago had brought back some sort of tension, some anger that bubbled beneath the skin like molten cheese sauce.

'Anyway,' Clementine said, settling slightly, 'I think your theory about the redevelopment is correct. When Arthur began his own investigation a few months back, he came and asked if he could look at the west wing before anyone started work.'

'You let him?'

'Of course I let him. Arthur almost died protecting Christopher. Even if he wasn't already a family friend, that would have settled things, don't you think?' Her eyes did the same twinkling thing as earlier, as though she were playing with Alice, testing her competence as a human being.

'Did he find anything?'

'He didn't say. Once he'd looked around, he came down for tea. We talked about how he was coping since Ethel's death. I offered to pay for a headstone. He didn't accept, and we left it at that.'

The three of them remained in silence, considering her words. Duke helped himself to the strange slice of pink cake that Clementine had left, as well as a few more that he said wouldn't be enough to feed a toddler, let alone a wedding party.

It was then that Alice saw it, on top of the mantelpiece behind Clementine and Duke. A large, black Jack Russell carved from resin. It had a few dings here and there but was otherwise in perfect condition. 'Just to go off topic, what's the story behind the dog up there?'

As Clementine turned around to look at the

ornament, another nostalgic smile touched her lips. 'One of my great-grandparents, I can't remember which, used to breed Jack Russells. This is all before the hunting ban, I'm sure. She produced such good dogs that a fellow huntsman commissioned a local factory to make her a pair of ornaments for the fireplace. The second one went missing years ago.'

Alice bared a triumphant grin. 'I think you might have just identified our murder weapon.'

'What have I told you about being dramatic?'

'You've room to talk,' Clementine said. 'You're one of the most dramatic men I've ever met, Marmaduke Featherstone.'

'So what do you think?' Alice asked.

'I think you're probably right.' Duke picked up his cup and bowled it in his hands. 'But that doesn't bring us any closer to finding the killer.'

Clementine rolled her eyes. 'See what I mean?'

Chapter Twenty

If the papers the next morning were anything to go by then their search for a killer was over. Alice checked her phone to find a voicemail message from her mother saying to check the news. A quick scroll through Facebook informed her that Bertram Sterling had confessed to the murder of Arthur and Ronnie. Sometime after she and Duke had visited the day before, he'd driven down to the police station and handed himself in. The officer tasked with speaking to the press said Bertram merely stated that the guilt of his crimes had become too heavy a burden to bear.

It may have only been half past seven, but Alice couldn't wait. She rang Jez. 'I need to talk to you about something,' she said as soon as he picked up, giving him no time to say hello.

'I'm in the living room.'

Alice froze with a hand in her matted hair. 'My living room?'

She heard movement downstairs, the sound of scuffing on the carpet. 'Yes, your living room,' he said. 'I thought you'd end up calling me, and here we are.'

'Does this count as breaking and entering?'

Jez laughed. 'Simply entering. You know the locks on these doors are no good.'

'Give me twenty minutes and I'll be down.'

'Twenty minutes?'

'Yes, Jez, women need time to get ready, you know?' She ended the call and climbed out of bed, grateful it was only Jez in her living room and not Ernie with the shaving rash.

Showered and dressed, Alice made her way downstairs to the living room.

Jez sat on the sofa, looking as pristine as ever.

'I swear your husband dresses you in the morning. You never looked this good at school,' she said, wandering through to the kitchen.

'That's because I was a teenage boy, not because I didn't have Ben to dress me. Besides, he was working late last night.'

Alice saw a full cup of tea beside the kettle. 'Is this for me?'

'I didn't have much else to do, so I thought I'd make a brew.' He shrugged.

'Practically poetry.' She walked back through and sat in the armchair across from him, setting her cup down on the coffee table.

Jez pointed towards the shopping bags lined up against the wall. 'You've got good wallpaper there. Why isn't it up yet?'

'That sounded almost like the beginnings of an interrogation, Jeremy.'

He shook his head, a smile on his face. 'It's Jez.'

'Is it? I didn't know.'

'I only asked about the wallpaper because I thought if you needed some help putting it up, Ben and I could come down and give you a hand.' He supped his drink, not meeting her gaze.

Alice smiled. 'If you make sure the pattern's straight and there are no cracks or bubbles, I'll make you a cake.'

His eyes lit up at this. 'What kind?'

'Whatever you like, within reason.'

'I'll speak to Ben, we'll sort something out.'

There was a nod from Alice, who said 'sounds like a plan' before adding, 'What can you tell me about Bertram Sterling?'

'Now who sounds like they're beginning an interrogation?'

'So?'

'There's not really much I can tell you outside of what we've already told the Gazette. Yesterday evening, he came to the station and told the duty officer he murdered Arthur and Ronnie.'

Alice allowed herself some time before responding, picking up her tea and swirling it around the cup. She inhaled a small amount of the steam that was left before glugging a mouthful, and then another mouthful, and then she swallowed the entire contents of the mug in her efforts to think about what Jez had told her. 'I just don't believe that of Bertram,' she said.

Jez had an almost consoling tone to his voice as he said, 'I understand that, Alice, but it just might fit.'

'How?

'Think of it from a police perspective and not as a civilian, for a moment. Bertram Sterling turns up at our door and confesses to the murder of his brother and friend. We can't take that lightly. It's an admission of guilt. That's the way things go, more often than not. Murder is a terrible practice and people can't handle committing it.

'You saw Bertram and Ronnie arguing, possibly about the armed robbery. We can't say for certain. Either way, what if Bertram killed Christopher in 1965 with the hopes of framing Ronnie? And what if Ronnie finds out and goes to argue with Bertram?

'We know Arthur was investigating the case. Perhaps he found the final piece of evidence he needed to confirm his brother was the murderer. Bertram, knowing his time is nearly up, silences them both with a murder weapon he's been hiding for fifty years.'

Alice remembered the grey pallor of Bertram's skin when she and Duke had been to visit. It didn't make sense that he'd kill his brother. Something niggled at the back of her mind, something Clementine had mentioned about Clive not being old enough to join the police force. 'How old is Bertram?'

Jez squinted at her. 'Sixty-four, I think.'

'Which would have made him fourteen at the time of Christopher's murder. Do you honestly believe a fourteen-year-old boy could commit murder and keep it secret this long?'

Surprise dawned on Jez's face. Alice watched it rise from his throat up, as though he was undergoing some sort of Power Rangers transformation. His mouth rounded, his cheeks rose, and the few wrinkles on his forehead furrowed. 'He never mentioned Christopher.'

'What?'

'We know that whoever killed Arthur and Ronnie also killed Christopher. Bertram hasn't mentioned Christopher's murder to any of our detectives.'

'You don't think he knows they're connected?'

He shook his head. 'Maybe he feels guilty about their deaths. Grief can do funny things to people.'

The front door flew open and slammed against the

wall.

Alice practically threw herself from the chair in shock, her heartbeat racing faster than a greyhound.

He rushed into the house, his eyes wild and a little bit bloodshot.

'Duke,' she exclaimed, 'what the bleeding heck do you think you're doing?'

'Sit down, Carson. You look a right plum.'

Jez had vaulted across the coffee table and now stood over Alice, as protective as a vegan over avocado. 'You're the one who just came in here looking like Freddie Kreuger on a bad day.'

That stopped Duke in his tracks. He cocked his head to the side and said, 'Really?'

Alice and Jez nodded.

A bevelled mirror hung on the wall beside the front door. Duke spun around and went to check his reflection. He pulled at the skin around his eyes and fussed with his hair, trying to make it look less like he'd just gone through a gorse bush at high speed. Once he was satisfied he'd got all the bits out of his teeth – a process that involved pressing his tongue against the gaps, as though a great pink slug were slithering over his gums – he returned to the front door and looked outside.

'Well come on then,' he said. 'It's not like we have all day.'

Alice shared a look with Jez and they watched the door, listening to the scuffing of shoes against the garden path, a slow desultory noise like a sloth with chronic fatigue. Eventually, Flora Sterling entered the house, looking a lot less forceful than she had the previous day. If anything, she was a perfect replica of her husband with her pale skin and eyes sinking back into her head, as though her skull wished to swallow them.

'Do you know why we're here?' Duke asked.

'It's a bit late for a slumber party, and I'm not cooking breakfast, so you must be here because Bertram has handed himself into the police despite the fact he isn't the killer.'

'Were you really a social worker?' Jez stared at her, flabbergasted.

Alice shrugged, nonchalant. 'There's maybe more than one reason I got sacked.'

'You agree with us then?' Flora spoke, a tremor to her voice that had gained a warble.

Jez spoke next, saying, 'I knew Alice would want to talk about it. She pointed out that Bertram only confessed to the murders of Arthur and Ronnie.'

'Aren't they the only murders?' Flora asked.

Duke placed a hand on her shoulder and leaned in close in what he clearly thought was consoling but which looked more as though he was about to devour her ear. 'They're the only people who've been killed recently, but whoever killed them is connected to the death of Christopher Partridge.'

'I need to sit down.' She pushed Duke away. Alice stood and offered her seat, thinking there was no way Flora would make it to the sofa.

'Jez make her a brew,' Alice said.

'It's your house.'

'And you're a police officer who broke into my house in the early hours of the morning. Make a bleeding drink. Lots of sugar.'

'I don't like sugar.'

'It's for shock. I'm not going in search of brandy at eight o'clock in the morning, so sweet tea will have to do.'

'You can be a bit mean, you know?'

Alice glanced across at a grinning Duke. 'I've been told.'

Whilst Jez busied himself making more drinks, Alice and Duke told Flora everything they knew about the murders; that Arthur, Ronnie, and Christopher were all killed with the same murder weapon, an ornament they believed had been hidden in a closed area of Greenfields before Clementine began her redevelopment; that Ronnie and Arthur were both killed in Arthur's cottage before the killer took Ronnie's body up to Brook Farm and tried to make it look like suicide, despite the fact that Ronnie's head had been caved in.

None of this seemed to help Flora, who still looked as though she was several inches away from collapsing outright across the coffee table. Alice had the good sense to remove the mugs and to reposition her magazines in case of any such fainting.

Flora took a cup of tea from Jez and thanked him with a nod of her head. She allowed herself a few sips before clearly thinking better of the idea and setting it down on the table. 'How exactly do we go about proving his innocence?'

'We're all on the same page. We'll go down to the station and speak to Clive,' Jez said, matter-of-factly.

'Will it work?'

'Of course, it'll work,' Duke said. 'They'll ask him questions, and when he can't answer them, they'll let him off.'

'I think we should consider why Bertram handed himself in. If he's grieving that badly, should we put him in touch with support groups and that sort of thing?'

Duke looked at Alice, his eyes as wide as a drugged-out owl. 'That might be the silliest idea you've ever had.'

'No,' she replied. 'That was letting you live here.'

He looked ready to say something more but thought better of it.

'She might be right, you know, Duke,' Flora said. 'You're thinking about this from a macho perspective. We all know the stigma against mental health issues, but if Bertie really is struggling then perhaps it would be best if he saw some sort of therapist.'

Jez didn't allow anyone else to talk. 'I think right now, the most important thing is making sure he gets home all right. Why don't we save all this until we can speak to him ourselves?'

'What if he can't cope with a huge crowd of people?' Flora asked.

'It would've been a bigger crowd in prison,' Alice said.

Jez sat down on the edge of the coffee table in front of Flora and brought himself to her level. When he spoke, there was a calm edge to his voice – soothing, almost. 'We're going to have more questions for him, Mrs Sterling. I know he's grieving the loss of his brother, but he still held up the investigation by lying to us. They might be lenient on him for wasting police time, but we still need to know what made him do so.'

Flora blanched even more, her head in her hands.

Alice and Duke glared at Jez. 'Couldn't that have waited for later?'

'I know I've been insensitive before, Jez, but really? That was too soon.'

'Let's go pick up Bertram,' he said.

Clive greeted them in reception. He didn't look happy. In fact, his brow furrowed so much that his wrinkles looked more like crevices on the huge mountain of his forehead.

Bertram sat on a plastic chair, nursing a cup of something brown and staring down at the stained floor tiles. Flora exclaimed his name and ran over to sit beside him, wrapping her arms around his shoulders, but he made no response.

'You're letting him off, then?' Duke said, taking charge.

'If I'd been on duty, the information wouldn't have been leaked to the press. But you know this town. The people are like vultures.' His glare reached Alice then. He clenched the back of Bertram's chair, his right hand a claw.

Clive turned his attention back to Duke and said, 'This is a serious case, Marmaduke. How you dare allow this girl to continue interfering is beyond belief.'

'She's competent, Clive.'

'You know the law. There's a reason why we don't let every Tom, Dick and Harry run about all over the place trying to solve crimes. She could be contaminating evidence and you wouldn't know until it was too late. Not only that, but it's ruddy dangerous. Look at Arthur. He thought he could solve this case, and now he's dead. Our original suspect is dead. There's a stranger out there who knows exactly what they're doing and before long your *assistant* here could very well be their next victim.'

Everyone in reception stared at Clive, agog. Apparently, the great daddy-long-legs wasn't prone to such outbursts. Not that you could tell. His face had turned a deep red, and his Adam's apple moved so quickly that it looked fit to burst through his throat.

'And you,' he yelled, at Jez now. 'You're supposed to still work for the police, aren't you? Do you think it's proper procedure to share confidential information about a case with a civilian?'

Jez didn't know what to say, so Alice stepped in saying, 'All right, mantis-man, take a deep breath before you have an asthma attack.' Clive made to reply, but she held her hand up to stop him. She shook her head. 'No. I might have paused for effect, but that doesn't give you permission to keep on acting the fool.'

Duke and Clive looked at one another, concern etched into the very marrow of their cheekbones.

'I'm twenty-five,' Alice said, 'and I recently discovered two dead bodies. Murder victims, you might say. Sure, I rang Duke first. Most would admit that they'd do strange things if they found a man with half his brains splattered across the mantelpiece like some new age Jackson Pollock painting. He's the one who contacted you. Both of you were friends with Arthur, I understand that. I wouldn't particularly want to see any of my long-term friends with their heads caved in, but I'd certainly have some sympathy for the person who did.

'You see, Clive…do you mind if I call you Clive? It doesn't matter either way, I just wanted to show you some common courtesy before I continued to say that I've felt guilt of which you probably can't imagine as you're such an upstanding member of the community.

'You have your sister in the big house on the hill. You've never had to worry about money, and your cousin was murdered fifty years ago. They never found his killer.

'You're on the police force, like your father before you. Presumably, you had some drive to find out just what happened to Christopher because you understand it was inhuman and vile, and you want his murderer, whoever they may be, brought to justice.

'I feel the same way about Arthur and Ronnie. If I'd let Duke stay in my cottage then he could have kept up surveillance and they'd still be alive. As it stands, I didn't, and now I need this murderer found because that's the only thing left I can do for them.'

Clive stammered, at a loss for words.

'It's still illegal to interfere in a police investigation, Alice,' Jez said.

She gritted her teeth. 'I know that, *Jeremy*, but I'm not having your boss talk about me like I'm not here.'

'He does that. He's Clive.'

Alice rolled her eyes and nodded towards Bertram. 'Is he free to go?'

'He never should have been here in the first place,' Clive said.

'At least we agree on something.' She turned back towards the door. 'Flora, grab your husband. We're going to Thistlethwaite's for a proper coffee.'

And then she walked out the building, leaving the others behind her.

Chapter Twenty-One

'That might be the most northern I've ever seen you,' Jez said, as they headed towards Thistlethwaite's Tea Room.

Alice shrugged. 'I'm from the north. It shouldn't be too much of a surprise.'

'But that was like, *proper* northern, like you were about to face down Tracy Barlow in Coronation Street.' He had a look of admiration that she hadn't seen on a man's face since she let Calvin Dodgson lick jam off her big toe. They'd split up after that. She didn't have a foot fetish and he'd never got over the aftertaste of her Dual Action Athlete's Foot Treatment Cream.

Jez held the door open for them, and they entered the café.

Mavis stood at the counter, hastily working a tea towel over a serving tray. She might have cried to Alice a few days earlier, but now she was back, looking as ferocious as ever. 'Morning,' she said, offering a smile that was one part homely, three parts terrifying.

'We'll have a latte, two teas, a cappuccino, and a flat white for Jez because he thinks he's being trendy,' Alice said, walking across to the biggest table.

'Is that all? I do serve food, you know. I'm not just some trendy coffee bar, hoping to appeal to would-be writers and yummy mummies. I have a business to run.'

Alice grinned. 'Better make it five full Englishes then, hadn't you?'

Mavis practically beamed at her. 'Good girl, I knew you weren't just a pretty face. You sit down and I'll bring them over.' She disappeared into the kitchen, followed by the sound of the coffee machine stuttering to work moments later.

'I'm surprised Clive let you off work after the way I spoke to him,' Alice said as they took their seats.

'I'm not off work, I'm just not due in yet.'

'Give the boy a break, Alice,' Duke said. 'You could have got him into a lot of trouble just now.'

She rolled her eyes at this. 'There'd be such a case of unfair dismissal that Partridge Mews would rock to its very core.'

'We're in Wren's Lea.'

Alice considered this for a moment. 'Fair point, well made.'

Bertram and Flora remained silent on the other side of the table, looking like a pair of desultory spaniels who'd just had their squeaky toy confiscated. They nestled together, Flora with her head on his shoulder, skin as ashen as ever.

Alice felt an ache in her chest to see them in such pain. The guilt she felt was difficult enough. She couldn't imagine how Arthur's own brother must be feeling. She thought back to the previous afternoon, questioning whether her words had been too harsh, whether she'd made too many jokes and ended up upsetting Bertram so much that he chose to hand himself into the police rather than face his grief.

She didn't have to wait for long. Before she knew it, Duke sat back in his chair and said to Bertram, 'Right then, lad, let's be having it. Why did you go and do something so stupid?'

'Duke!' At least Flora's outrage put some colour in her cheeks.

Bertram patted his wife's shoulder. 'It's all right, Flo. Let Duke ask his questions.'

'Are you sure?' Alice asked, eliciting a look from Duke which told her to keep out of it.

Bertram nodded. 'It's simple enough, really. I'm guilty.'

'Come off it. We already know that's not true.'

'I'll admit I didn't kill either of them, but I *am* guilty.' He sighed from the depths of his lungs and said, 'I'm the one who framed Ronnie for the armed robbery.'

Alice looked to Duke, who looked to Jez, who looked to Alice, who looked to Bertram.

'Mr Sterling,' Jez said. 'You do understand the severity of your admission?'

If anything, Bertram looked more relaxed. Some tension had left his shoulders as he met Jez's gaze. 'I know what I did was wrong, but I had my reasons.'

'Would you care to go into them now?'

'Not here,' he said. 'All I'll say is that there's folk who knew someone had it in for Christopher Partridge, and they were all set to put Ronnie in the frame.'

'So, you stole his gun?' Alice asked.

The kitchen door opened, and Mavis came out with her tray loaded up. She moved towards them as poised and determined as a shark after a surfer, setting their drinks down in the centre of the table and handing them out.

The five of them offered their thanks as they took

their cups off her.

When she'd finished handing them out, Mavis walked back towards the kitchen. 'Bear in mind, Bertram, these walls are thin. You might not see me, but as sure as the Lord's name is Jehovah, I can hear you.' She let the door swing shut behind her, the scent of bacon wafting towards them.

'That settles it, then,' Bertram said. 'I suppose I haven't really got anything to lose. She'll tell half the town before we've even left here.'

Alice stirred her latte. 'That's exactly why I brought you here.'

Flora looked at her, aghast. 'Are you completely out of touch with reality?'

'People are going to gossip no matter what. They trust Mavis. She can tell them that Bertram didn't kill Arthur or Ronnie. When they hear he even chose her café for his post-jail breakfast, she won't let them say a word against him.'

Flora backed down. 'I suppose that makes sense.'

Alice offered her a smile. Meanwhile, she was worried about her second full English in as many days, wondering if she was slowly replacing Pinot Grigio with fatty foods and carbohydrates. She didn't imagine it was possible to gain several stone in a week, but she knew hers would be the body to do it, out of spite more than anything.

Bertram poured a large quantity of sugar into his tea, then made a meal out of stirring it, as though he wanted to be certain each and every granule had dissolved. Eventually, he sat back in his seat and said, 'I did steal Ronnie's gun.'

'Did you plan how you'd frame him?'

'Ronnie had previous. He was always getting into

trouble for something. If it wasn't poaching, it'd be sheep rustling. He always had a get rich quick scheme in his head. I suppose that's why the lads thought it'd be easy to frame him.'

'What lads are these, then?' Duke asked, half his tea still dribbling from his stubble.

'I can't name names, Duke. Not yet.' Bertram closed his eyes, the confession taking its toll on him. 'They were always going on about what a toff Christopher was and how someone should knock him down a peg or two. Then one of them caught onto the idea that Ronnie was such a scumbag that they'd be able to frame him for it. We were only teenagers. I thought it was all talk, what lads do. Then it started to get serious. They started coming up with plans. Stealing Ronnie's gun and shooting Christopher. Making it a proper job.

'When Ronnie reported his gun missing, I knew where to look. I cycled over in the middle of the night. Arthur thought I was off to meet some girl. I brought the gun home and hid it in my Dad's shed. We were forever hiding things in there. I'm pretty sure I lost a couple of army men once.'

'You didn't steal the gun from Ronnie?' Jez asked, beating Alice and Duke to the punch.

Bertram shook his head. 'No. I knew when they planned to kill Christopher, so I took the gun to the jewellers, smashed a window and left the gun. Then I went down the road to a telephone box and reported the robbery myself.'

Alice couldn't believe what she was hearing. Bertram felt guilty because he *was* guilty. He might have saved Ronnie from being done for murder, but he'd still lost him the love of his life. 'You knew they were going to kill Christopher and rather than protect him, you chose to protect Ronnie. Why?'

He looked to Flora. She had tears in her eyes that she'd tried to mop up with a napkin, leaving her face flaky and red.

Bertram faced Alice and said, 'I'm going to share a secret now that only Flora knows about and only Flora needs to know about. If this goes any further than this café, I'll go straight to the police and report the lot of you for harassment. Do you understand?' He looked vicious, as though he'd happily impale their nostrils on teaspoons.

'You've no need to worry about us, Bertie,' Duke said. 'I'll make sure no one hears what you've got to say.'

'Well, all right then. The thing is, I'm what you might call bisexual. I know the "in thing" nowadays is to be out and proud, but it was different when I was a kid and you simply didn't go around telling folk you liked lads and lasses.'

Jez swallowed hard and said, 'That's your business, Mr Sterling, but we respect you for telling us.'

Alice quirked an eyebrow towards Jez. 'That's all you have to say?'

'What else should I say?'

'Sure, it was supportive, but you could have told him that you're married to a man and that you're the least likely person to judge him.'

'I could have, but I didn't.'

Mavis came back with food for them then, bearing another tray upon which sat plates packed with an inordinate number of greasy delights. Bacon, sausages, eggs and mushrooms, all fried, all dripping with fat, then the fried bread, hash browns and toast. The tomatoes were the healthiest things on the plates, and even they looked like they'd been injected with extra cholesterol. These full English breakfasts were every dietician's worst nightmare packed onto one serving tray, and it made Alice's stomach rumble to see it.

Mavis grinned at Bertram as she set his plate down in front of him. 'I won't tell anyone this bit of business, Bertie, don't you worry. I want them to catch Arthur's killer as much as the next person.' She set her hand on his shoulder, sniffed, and walked away, dabbing her eyes on her tea-towel.

Bertram stared after her, a slight wobble to his lips, barely there, as though they had a wasp sting stuck in them. He poured salt and pepper over his eggs and mushrooms and tucked in.

That's how they remained for a few minutes, each of them chewing, swallowing, and mulling over the new information that Bertram had given them. Alice was reminded of Christopher and Ronnie keeping their relationship a secret all those years before. It had been a different world, one in which her mother was still a toddler and her father wasn't yet a twinkle in his father's eyes. With Bertram's words in mind, she said, 'I hope this isn't the wrong way to go about things, but were you and Ronnie in a relationship?'

Bertram had just been spooning baked beans onto his fried bread when she asked. The question brought a smile to his face, which soon evolved into a chuckle. 'No, Ronnie and I weren't in a relationship. I was fourteen and he was in his early twenties. Ronnie used to come and help on the farm during the summertime. We grew close and I realised I had feelings for him. I fancied him, but it was nothing more than a schoolboy crush. He never even knew.' This last sentence brought a glimmer of sadness to his face, not unnoticed by Flora who took his hand in hers.

'Bertie has always been perfectly honest with me about his sexuality. Like he said, it's never been anyone else's business. When Ronnie came back to take over Brook Farm, he came looking to see if we could give him a hand getting the place up and running. We did, and we became closer friends because of it.'

'Do you still have feelings for Ronnie?' Duke asked, choosing to take the more difficult question for himself.

'Only as a friend, Duke, if you'll believe that.'

Alice and Jez both looked at Bertram's face to see if there was some secret there beneath his answer, but no. He was a man riddled with grief.

'You know that folk believe he was having an affair with Flora,' Alice said.

Bertram nodded. 'What does it matter what other people think? I let him come and do some extra work at the farm because of my arthritis and, if anything, I don't think I'll ever stop feeling guilty about what happened.'

'You were a teenager in love. We all do stupid things.'

'Writing soppy poems, maybe. Not getting a man killed. I have the deaths of three men on my conscience.' He shook his head and gulped down some fried bread.

'It would really help the police if you told us who you're protecting,' Jez said.

'It was your job to protect Christopher Partridge, and look how good a job you did there.' Bertram stared Jez dead in the eyes and said, 'That's all I'm saying. I thought I knew who killed Christopher, but he had an alibi. I'm guilty of framing Ronnie Butterworth for an armed robbery that never happened when I was fourteen years old. Either arrest me or leave me alone, because that's all I'm saying on the matter.'

'You can't force him to talk,' Duke said.

'You're not wrong.'

'He might not be able to,' Alice said. 'But I want to know if you're feeling so guilty about your brother's death, why won't you tell us who killed him?'

'That's simple. I told Ronnie who might've killed Christopher, he told Arthur, and now they're both dead. This isn't secrecy. This is self-preservation.'

Alice stared at him. Anger coiled in her stomach, winding its way into her clenched fists and fierce glare. 'This is what you were arguing about in the shop, isn't it? You told Ronnie who killed Christopher and he wanted to go to the police.'

Bertram looked down at his plate.

'I think that's enough. Bertie's said all he has to say.' Flora had cleaned up her plate, worry having done nothing to her appetite.

'That's not enough actually, Flo,' Alice said, as she recalled Bertram's argument with Ronnie, 'because your husband said they couldn't go to the police because Ronnie had previous for armed robbery. An armed robbery that never happened and which he knew Ronnie didn't commit. You never told Ronnie it was you, did you?'

'How do you tell someone you helped ruin their life?'

'There's a reason you feel guilty, Bertram, and that's because you are. You might not have committed murder, but you bleeding helped.'

Flora glowered at Alice as though she could melt her with her eyes. 'How dare you? Don't you think he's been through–'

'If you say "enough", I swear I'll throw a grilled

tomato at you so hard you'll have vines growing where your retinas should be.'

'To think I gave you a free breakfast yesterday.'

'It should've been free, the state of it.'

'Well you certainly won't be having one again.'

'Good, I'll stick to Thistlethwaite's. At least here you aren't being served by a serial killer's assistant.' The venom in Alice's tone was so vicious it could've burned holes in Bakelite.

Bertram stared at her, dumbstruck. He stood up, followed shortly by Flora, leaving the three of them behind.

'That really didn't go well, did it?' Jez necked his flat white.

Duke had his eyes on Bertram's half-finished breakfast. He grinned at Alice. 'If he's not going to have it, I might as well.'

Alice took slow, deep breaths, focusing on her mother's teachings. Yet the fury continued to gurgle unbridled within her. 'You might be right, you know, Duke.'

'What's that?'

'There's a chance I'm a hot-head.'

'Oh, that. I shouldn't worry too much. You only said what we were thinking.'

Alice finished the rest of her breakfast in silence, too annoyed to care if it affected her waistline. She felt an apology wedge in her throat like forgotten chewing gum. She had nothing to say to the Sterlings, only Mavis; Alice had spouted vitriol that definitely shouldn't be spoken in the presence of lace doilies.

She knew the guilt that came with grief and had hoped by inflicting that on Bertram, he would reveal his suspicions. Rather than find a killer, she'd ended up finding herself new enemies.

Chapter Twenty-Two

That afternoon, Marmaduke and Alice sat in his garden, going over her harsh words with Flora, Duke's main concern being that Alice might have cost him his breakfasts. She made sure that her look was equal parts furious and gleeful as she said, 'How did you last so long as a detective if all it takes to get you onside is a well-cooked sausage?'

'You agree her food is good, then?'

'I said it was well-cooked. That says nothing about flavour or texture, simply that she knows how to use a hob.' She'd just settled down in the grass when they heard someone yell Duke's name from the front door.

'What does he want?' Duke grumbled. He attempted to get out of his sun lounger, only for Clive to show up at the back door.

'I did try knocking,' he said. He took off his hat and placed it on the bird table.

'Rather than take the hint you're not wanted here, you thought you'd mosey on in?' Duke settled back down and put his sunglasses on.

'The door was open.'

'To let some fresh air flow through, not some

walloping great matchstick man who calls himself a detective.'

'Matchstick man?' Alice asked.

'You know, because of the long legs and dangly arms.'

'Ah, I thought daddy-long-legs.'

'I believe you called me mantis-man, referencing the insect,' Clive stated, his haughty tones setting Alice on edge.

'Thank you for remembering my insult, Detective Constable. It makes it much easier for me in future.'

'It's Detective Inspector Constable, really.'

'Is it?' Alice pulled her phone out and began scrolling through Facebook, refusing to give Clive the attention he craved. Of course, she knew her mother would admonish her for being mean to her elders – she dreaded to think what Primrose would say about her treatment of the Sterlings – but Alice had always found it difficult to hold her tongue. It had been the same as long as she could remember.

During her school's Christmas Pageant in 1998, she'd been tasked with carrying the Baby Jesus onto the stage. Naturally, overcome with nerves, she dropped the doll. Afterwards, Eloise Bellflower said *she* wouldn't have dropped the baby because she had a younger sister and her Mum always let Eloise carry her. At which point, Alice said it was a pity someone wasn't around to stop Eloise's Mum from dropping her. This then led to several remarks about Eloise having a nose like a squashed tomato and Alice having to attend fortnightly meetings with the headmistress about bullying.

Aunty Magdalena, meanwhile, praised Alice's wit and bought her a new scooter for Christmas. Alice tried to recall which husband Aunty Magdalena had been with at the time, but it became too difficult. There'd been that short period with Hugo who kept trying to make a duck bill out of Pringles, but she had no idea if he'd been around for Christmas.

Alice wasn't really listening to Clive and Duke's discussion. It had started with some apology for the way Clive had spoken that morning, before he went on to say, 'It's a stressful time, Duke. I'm nearly at retirement age. When I first joined the force, they thought I'd be the one to solve the heir's murder where my father hadn't.'

'How many times have I told you? You can't go about life trying to live up to Creswell's legacy.' He managed to sit up then, pulling himself to the end of his sun lounger.

This piqued Alice's interest. She stopped reading about how Lucy Webb was making money peddling diet shakes to her friends and relatives to watch the exchange between the two of them.

Clive scratched the back of his head, putting the wispy white weeds into disarray. 'I know what you mean, but it's a difficult situation. Christopher was my brother-in-law. I owe it to Clementine to find out who killed him.'

Duke nodded and smacked his lips together. 'I'll give you that, it's not easy, but there's no use getting too emotional. What do the forensics say?'

'There are no fingerprints. All we know is it's the same murder weapon and there are some fibres on it.'

'Tweed,' Alice said.

A moment of shock passed across Clive's face before settling into mere acknowledgement. 'That's right. You've been talking to Detective Carson, I see. I'll be having words with him.'

Alice rolled her eyes. 'You just told Duke, in front of me, that you'd found fibres. I happened to say what those fibres could be, and you confirmed it. You'd be better off having words with yourself.'

'You've quite the tongue on you, haven't you?'

'And you've quite the forehead, but I didn't think it polite to say.' Alice looked down at her phone, ending the conversation.

'Don't mind her,' Duke said. 'She's one of these modern women.'

Alice avoided responding and read all about the benefits of replacing three meals a day with two powder shakes – SlimFast in sheep's clothing – and a calorie-reducing tablet. For just a few hundred pounds, she could say no to Pinot Grigio and hello to smoothies that looked more like cold concrete.

She scrolled on.

'I really did just come to apologise, Duke,' Clive said. 'Things have been tough, and when Bertram came to the police station, it really riled me up. We all know he'd never harm Arthur like that. And that's besides the fact he had no idea we'd connected it to the death at Greenfields.'

'It's fine, Clive. I understand. Tell you what, why don't we go down the Harrington one night and toast Arthur's memory? Has his son been in touch about the body yet?'

'Ian? No. As far as we know, he's still in New Zealand. We tried getting in touch with Arthur's grandson, Luke, but he's in Rotherham undercover.'

This interested Alice. She had fond memories of Luke and remembered the way his muscles moved as he mowed Arthur's front garden. His biceps were sinuous enough to cause the heartbeat of any teenager to flutter. She'd wondered just where Luke had got to. She understood that things could have changed between him and his grandfather in the seven years since she last saw him, but she thought Arthur's death would have brought him back to Partridge Mews.

'He's doing well for himself, then?'

'He's still on the force, if that's what you mean.'

'I get what you're saying.' Duke nodded solemnly.

Alice knew to keep her curiosity to herself. She endeavoured to look as though she was focused on her phone, and the topless picture someone had posted of Liam Hemsworth – definitely not something she wanted to be caught looking at in Duke's back garden. She scrolled down fast until she reached a less incriminating post. Not that there was anything worth seeing on Facebook. It only served as a free record of all the stupid things her former classmates got up to, and that included the regular births, deaths and marriages.

'Anyway,' Clive said, 'I only called to make sure things are all right between us. I'd best be getting home, Helena's making a casserole and she wants me to pick up the wine.'

'Tell her I said hello.'

Clive nodded as he headed back inside.

'Clive!' Duke called.

He turned back, startled, wondering just what he'd done now.

'Hat.' Duke pointed at the trilby sat on the bird table.

Clive calmed instantly and shook his head. Chuckling, he picked up his hat, thanked Duke, and left them to their own devices.

'And let me know about that drink,' Duke shouted

after him.

Alice froze where she sat, her stomach gurgling as she recalled the day she'd found Arthur's body. Hoping her memory was wrong, she turned off Facebook and found the photos she had of Arthur's house.

Although she'd taken the photos with the flash on, they were still too dark for her to see anything fully. Her stomach ached to see Arthur sprawled across his chair, eyes glazed over, looking like he belonged in a horror flick, the victim of some real villain.

Alice scrolled through the photos, following the blood spatters and the possible brain matter she really hoped was a vampiric dust bunny, until she found what she was looking for.

She zoomed in on a hat on the floor, a tweed trilby that was an exact replica of the one Clive had just picked up off the bird table.

She looked up at Duke, who was sitting content in his sun lounger, feeling better for reconciling things with an old friend.

'Clive wasn't wearing his hat, Duke,' she said, her mouth dry.

'Eh?' he said. 'What are you talking about? He just picked it up.'

'On the day of Arthur's murder, when he turned up at the house, he wasn't wearing his hat.'

She hadn't expected the rising tension in Duke's shoulders, the growl in his voice as he said, 'I'd be careful what you're saying, Alice. I know you believe you're helping but think about this.'

'Another officer came running out of the house to give it to him.'

'It must've fallen out of his pocket when we were looking at Arthur.'

Alice held the picture of her phone up. 'Clive's hat is in the pictures I took for you, before either of you arrived.'

'Then he must have left it when he last saw Arthur. They were friends, you know.'

'Duke, we have to think about this.'

'No, we don't!' he exclaimed, tearing his sunglasses from his face and dropping them to the ground to show Alice the full measure of his disgust. 'Clive is a friend of mine, and Arthur's. Do you honestly think I'm going to believe he's a murderer?'

Alice swallowed hard, forcing back the lump in her throat. 'But he could be. He's connected to all three murders.'

He was on his feet now, no need for a comedic struggle from a sun lounger. 'So am I. So are half the people in this town. Anyone who happened to be at the fete in 1965 and is still living could be the murderer, so why have you chosen Clive? Because of his hat? Or because you don't like him?'

She pocketed her phone and walked back into her house.

'We're not done here!'

She took her keys off the kitchen counter, then walked through the hall with its dusty bin bags and out the front door.

She listened to Duke rushing through the house, brushing against everything. He stopped at the front door to say, 'Alice, I'm warning you, this is the wrong path to go down. If you accuse Clive, I don't think we can continue this partnership.'

Alice stopped at her car. 'This isn't a partnership. This is two people feeling guilty for the death they helped to cause. If you don't want to listen to me, fine.

I'm not a detective. I'm not a social worker. I'm nothing.'

'Is this what you do? Throw your toys out the pram when you're wrong.'

She smiled at him. 'Goodbye, Duke. I hope you find your answers.' She got into the car and drove away, putting all thoughts of Marmaduke Featherstone to the back of her mind.

Chapter Twenty-Three

After one bottle of Pinot Grigio, she wanted to track down Clive and prove she hadn't been wrong. After two bottles, she began to question his motives. She had no idea why Clive would kill Christopher Partridge. The third and fourth bottles put her in a drunken stupor, paralytic almost, as she turned to Netflix and season five of RuPaul's Drag Race.

Alice didn't remember much after that.

She awoke to the sound of someone banging against the front door with so much force she envisaged the Incredible Hulk with a battering ram.

Her head throbbed, making pins from her eyes as she squinted them open.

The first thing she realised was that she wasn't in bed. Nor was she in the bathroom, holding the toilet tight against her chest and praying for the sweet mercy of death to come and save her from a hangover.

No, at some point during the night, a rather drunken Alice had dragged the armchair across the living room, squeezed it into the hall, and used it to block the front door. Then she'd collapsed against it, her legs in the doorway of the living room and her neck angled against the chair, in just the right position for cold air to blow against her midriff.

'Alice!'

Jez continued to hammer against the door.

'I'm right here,' she said, her voice as rough as gorse.

He stopped. 'Did you say something?'

The door was slightly ajar. She spoke up. 'I may have had too much wine.'

'You're behind the door?'

'As is the armchair.'

'Do I need to get help?'

Alice grabbed hold of the chair's arm and dragged herself to her feet. She rubbed at the ache in her neck, regret as immediate as the room spinning. 'I'm assessing the situation,' she said, as nausea threatened to cause all manner of distress to her body.

The chair was wedged against the wall, having been pushed further by Jez's attempts to get inside.

She pushed the door shut and dragged the armchair back, heaving and twisting it through the living room door and back inside.

Once it was out of the way, Jez opened the door and entered the cottage, helping her to put the chair back in its rightful place.

'You really went to town, didn't you?' he said, surveying the damage.

Alice couldn't remember how the living room had got into disarray, but the coffee table lay on its side, with the sofa cushions behind it and a duvet cover over the lot of it. 'I think I was building a fort.'

Jez struggled to contain a grin. 'Any idea why?'

'There's a strong possibility I ended up watching *The Walking Dead.*'

'Zombie apocalypse?'

Alice nodded. She crossed the living room into the kitchen and opened the fridge to retrieve her phone. Pressing the cold device against her forehead, she retrieved paracetamol from a cupboard and switched on the kettle.

'Why was your phone in the fridge?'

'I'm beggared if I know.' She got herself a glass of water and necked the paracetamol.

'I came to let you know that Bertram and Flora have left town. They say the stress of everything has taken its toll and they need to leave for their health.'

'Good to know.' Alice recalled her words to Flora and winced. Ordinarily, she'd have felt some pride at talking someone down, but now something akin to guilt rose up in her chest, merging with that she felt at Arthur's death, her last conversation with Duke, and that time she'd stolen Gabe Yearsly's Charizard.

Jez leant down on the kitchen counter, his head cocked to the side. 'So, what's the reason behind your binge drinking?'

'Binge drinking? Where do you get that idea from?'

'I've stepped over six empty Pinot Grigio bottles to stand here.'

'Oh. How do you know I wasn't drinking with Duke?'

'He calls wine "gnat's water".'

Alice started making herself a cup of coffee, and a tea for Jez. 'All right then,' she said. 'Duke and I had a little disagreement.'

'A little disagreement caused you to drink enough alcohol to render a rhinoceros catatonic?'

'Those words are much too big to use this early in the morning.'

'It's half past one in the afternoon.'

Alice put her head in her hands and groaned. 'Why am I such a terrible adult?'

'If I had to choose anything, I'd blame your upbringing,' he said, a smile creeping in.

'You're not wrong.' She handed him his drink and sidled into the living room, sitting in the armchair that wasn't quite in its right place because she couldn't bring herself to move it. She also found herself aware she was wearing pyjamas with no idea when they'd found their way onto her body, but they were definitely pyjamas and they definitely had Christmas reindeer on them.

Once more, Jez took the seat across from her. Perhaps this was the way of things now, Jez turning up at the cottage and questioning her in the living room. 'Do I need to ask what you and Duke disagreed about?'

'You kind of just did.'

'Well?'

Alice couldn't meet his gaze directly, choosing to look instead at the kitchen window far behind him. 'I think I've found our killer.'

'And Duke thinks differently?'

'I think if it was anyone else, he would have thought about it, but because I say it's Clive, he won't listen to me.'

'You think Clive killed Arthur and Ronnie?' There was an air of disappointment to Jez's tone.

Alice found the photograph on her phone again and handed it over. 'It's all to do with his hat. When Clive turned up at Arthur's cottage, he wasn't wearing his hat because his hat was inside already.'

Jez gave his best attempt of looking at the photo before returning her phone.

'You don't believe me.'

'Whoever killed Arthur also killed Christopher. Clive

would've been fourteen at the time. You said it yourself yesterday morning, you don't believe a teenager could have kept murder a secret this long.'

'I was talking about Bertram.'

'Who's the same age as Clive.'

Alice rubbed at her forehead, trying to alleviate some of the throbbing above the bridge of her nose. 'Bertram said he knew the boys who planned to kill Christopher. What if Clive is the one who came up with the plan?'

'We have it on good authority that Clive was in a police car at the time, outside an armed robbery. His father thought that if someone was after Christopher, they'd be after the whole family.'

'Clive's father?'

'I think you've forgotten that he oversaw the original investigation.'

'Giving him a better chance of being able to cover it up. The west wing of Greenfields has been closed since the Second World War. Did they search there in 1965?'

'As a matter of fact, they did, and they didn't find anything.'

'I thought we were sure that's where he hid the weapon.'

'Don't say "he", just because you've made the decision that it was Clive.' Jez sounded stern, worse than any father telling his child off. 'You can't go around making accusations, Alice. This is a serious business, and you'll only put the case in jeopardy if you continue to do so.'

Alice felt her heart sink further into her stomach. She hadn't expected Jez to believe his superior officer capable of murder, but at least he hadn't grown as furious as Duke. 'Maybe you're right,' she said. 'I suppose I got caught up in the idea of catching a killer without giving any thought to how I'd affect people.'

'You're apologising?'

She nodded. 'I'm leaving this to the professionals.'

'What will you do in the meantime?' He didn't say he thought it for the best, but she could tell he approved of her decision.

'I think I'm going to take myself off to bed and then go see my Mum.'

'That sounds like a good idea.' He stood up and made his way over to the front door. 'It's brave to admit when you've got it wrong, Alice. Don't hide in here too long.'

She didn't face him, didn't want to show him the tide of tears brimming in her eyes. Tears that, when Jez shut the front door, Alice let run free.

Chapter Twenty-Four

Alice spent the rest of her day lounging about the house feeling sorry for herself. Her hangover didn't alleviate, and despite considering going to her parents' house she realised she'd much rather spend her time at the cottage and wallow in self-pity, nausea and enough toast to feed an entire hut of Scouts.

She found a Spotify playlist of sad songs and listened to them whilst she was in the bath. A bath she lingered in a lot longer than normal, adding more hot water, letting the skin on her fingertips shrivel until she could see faces in the wrinkles.

Something ate away at her insides and left her feeling hollow. She couldn't help but feel that if she didn't find out who killed Arthur then she was letting him down. She supposed that was her guilt talking. Yet the more she thought about it, the more she questioned whether Duke's presence at the cottage had anything to do with protecting Arthur at all, or whether the time of Arthur's death and Duke's departure had simply been an unfortunate coincidence.

No one disputed that Clive's hat was beside Arthur's corpse. They just denied he killed Arthur. It made sense. Arthur had presumably worked with Clive for years and had even been his superior officer at one time or another. There would have been plenty of opportunity to kill him over the years.

Except there had never been any need.

Whoever killed Christopher Partridge needn't worry because nobody bothered with the case. Yet in his final months, Arthur grew determined and set out to find a murderer. A murderer whose identity his brother knew.

She supposed no one could force Bertram to tell them who he was protecting. It could only be supposition. A group of young lads all planning to murder Christopher Partridge because of his social status – any one of them could be the killer, and Alice hadn't the slightest idea who they were, but she knew someone who would.

The next morning, she turned up at Thistlethwaite's before Mavis even arrived.

It had been a strange night. She knew she'd managed to sleep because of a dream she'd had involving baked Alaska and a trip to the moon on a bowl of Coco Pops. She'd also been kept awake half the night, theorising over the murders.

Mavis eventually appeared at the end of the road. She walked along at her normal pace, refusing to acknowledge Alice's presence until she'd unlocked the door. 'Your mother says you're good with a kettle. You'd better get inside and start brewing up if you fancy asking me any questions.'

Alice stood beside the doorway whilst Mavis went into the kitchen to switch on the lights. She tossed an apron to Alice and tied her own around her waist. 'I don't suppose that Marmaduke sent you, did he?' Mavis asked, as shrewd as an owl over a dormouse.

'We fell out.'

'I knew you would.' Mavis led Alice into the kitchen and pointed her in the direction of the teapot. 'You can make a brew whilst I get the bacon out the freezer. Jack Lindsay will be here dead on eight o'clock, and he likes his fat crispy.'

Alice made the tea and they took it through to the café.

'Now, what do you want to ask me?' Mavis asked.

'It's to do with the murder.'

'Naturally. You wouldn't be waiting on my doorstep to ask after my scone recipe, would you?' Mavis sniggered at her own joke and went about adding milk and sugar to her own cup. It seemed she had quite the sweet tooth from the way she heaped the sugar onto the spoon, almost willing it to accept more granules.

'I think you heard me shout at Bertram and Flora the other day.'

'It wasn't your finest hour, but you'd think Bertram would tell the police who killed his brother.'

'Right.' Alice gulped. 'The thing is, I believe the killer is a member of the police.'

Mavis's eyes became slits as she leaned in close. 'Who?'

'Clive Constable.'

Mavis guffawed. She flew back in her chair, nearly knocking herself to the ground. 'Clive Constable? You never?'

'You heard Bertram yesterday, he was part of a group of lads who planned to kill Christopher Partridge.'

'Yes, but it wouldn't have been Clive, his sister was married to the man.' Mavis shook her head and dabbed at her cheeks with a tea towel. 'That's made my morning, that has. You must be rubbish at Cluedo.'

Alice felt sick with embarrassment. She turned away from Mavis and rested her back against the wall, staring out the window at the street as it slowly came to life. This must have been the sight Arthur saw every morning before he came to work. He'd had that taken away from him, and no one would take her seriously.

'There's no need to laugh, Mavis Thistlethwaite,' she practically growled. 'I'm trying to find out who murdered your assistant and friend, if you'd failed to notice.'

Mavis placed her hands on top of Alice's and said, 'I know it's difficult, Alice, but I simply can't see Clive killing anybody.'

'All right then. Who are the other boys that Bertram and Clive hung around with?'

Mavis rubbed her chin, as though it was a magic trick for summoning memory. 'Let's see, there was Alfie Booth, but he's dead. Same goes for Cyril, John, and Edward. I think Michael Carnegie moved to Aberystwyth after his marriage broke down, and that's about it, really.'

Alice stared at Mavis, her lips parted, eyes agog. 'What you're telling me is that out of the group of boys that could have killed Christopher, the majority is dead, one is in Wales, and the only two remaining as suspects couldn't have killed him in the first place?'

Mavis nodded. 'Think about it. Young lads talk about doing stupid stuff all the time, but they rarely follow through with it. The fact of the matter is that although Bertram heard his mates talking about killing someone, they were probably nowhere near Greenfields when Christopher was killed.'

'The police records say Clive was under protection as well, at the time. He was taken down to Partridge Mews and left in a police car, supposedly out of harm's way.' Alice shook her head.

'That's right, the police were asked to guard the place because they'd received some threats of violence. Although I thought they'd solved all that in the end.' She slurped her tea whilst it was hot before pouring herself another cup.

'No one's ever told me they solved it.'

'Isobel Ramsbottom it was, causing trouble again as usual. She had a very pious father, poor girl, and he blamed Christopher for Isobel's unwanted pregnancy. He sent letter after letter to Greenfields, threatening him. In the end, Isobel had a falling out with one of her "friends" who revealed that he was the baby's father, and that she'd never even met Christopher, they just thought they'd make a quick buck. Isobel's father apologised for the letters.'

'But Christopher was already dead?'

'It surprises me that no one questioned Isobel about the murder.'

'Maybe because they already knew who the killer was.'

'Don't start on that again. You're barking up the wrong tree, I tell you.'

'That may be so, and if I'm proved wrong, I'll apologise.' Alice cradled her tea in her hands. Nothing Mavis said made her doubt Clive could be a killer. If anything, it only strengthened her resolve. Now, she just needed evidence.

Chapter Twenty-Five

Alice stayed at Thistlethwaite's to help out with the morning shift. One of Mavis's younger relatives came to help her out in the afternoon. He arrived in suit jacket and trousers, clearly dressing for the job he wanted rather than the job he had. Mavis introduced him as Theo, thanked her for helping out, and Alice left, glad to be away. She swore the smell of cooking fat would linger in her hair for days to come, no matter how much conditioner she used.

She went to her parents' house in the hope of seeing her mother. Instead, she found Norman in the front room, connecting a wire from his helmet-cam to his laptop.

She sat down next to him on the sofa and said, 'Mum won't be happy if she sees you with your feet on the table.'

'I won't say anything if you don't.'

Alice followed her father's lead and put her legs up too. 'Are you two still arguing?'

'Let's just say your mother hasn't quite got her head around the idea that I'll be going away for a month.'

'You're definitely planning on going, then?'

'You understand, don't you?'

'I understand you're trying to get out of helping me decorate the cottage.' Alice leant on Norman's shoulder, snuggling against him. 'I think I found the killer, Dad.'

'Is this good or bad news?'

'Duke doesn't agree.'

'So you came here for some fatherly support?'

'That was two days ago. He got angry. I drank a few bottles of wine, slept it off, went to see Mavis and now I'm here.' Alice pressed against her father's side until he set his laptop down and wrapped his arms around her. 'Now you're taking the hint,' she said, shifting to nestle her head against his chest.

Norman placed his chin on top of her head, holding her close to him as he'd done since she was a toddler with a fear of swans coming to kidnap her in her sleep.

Alice listened to her father's heartbeat, his pulse as soothing to her as lullabies had once been. In these moments, she lingered in his arms, forgot about the world and her troubles, and simply existed. Here, she felt calm. The aching tension in her forehead slipped away and before she knew it, she fell asleep.

She awoke in the same position. Norman took his fatherly duties seriously. Alice might have been twenty-five years old, but he followed the same mantra as if she were a baby – if she was asleep and even the slightest movement could wake her, he didn't move. At least he had the remote to hand, because Alice opened her eyes to him incorrectly answering questions to The Chase. 'Shakespeare didn't write Carry on Cleo, Dad.'

'I wondered if it might have been a spoof.' He shrugged. 'Did you sleep well?'

Alice yawned but remained where she lay. 'I think

so.'

'I think so, too. It's been a fair few hours, you must've needed it.'

'I might have been a bit excessive with the Pinot Grigio the other day.'

'Your Mum will be home soon. Why don't you stick around for tea?'

'As long as it's not a repeat of the last time. I don't want you two arguing about how many nappies you changed in 1991.'

'Good, because I lost count.'

Alice sat up, allowing Norman to stretch out his arm. She caught sight of herself in the reflection from the television and attempted to fix her hair. 'Did you mess with my hair again?'

Norman shook his head. 'You still fidget in your sleep.'

'I look like something out of a Western.' She ran her hands through her hair, wincing at the pain as she tugged on knots and pulled at the giant brunette tumbleweed on top of her head.

'I tell you what. You go to your room and figure out how to fix your hair, and I'll make some hot chocolate.'

'You're really trying to score Dad points, aren't you?'

He chuckled and stood up. 'I don't need to score Dad points. I already won. I'm the front runner in the race of best fathers.'

'How did you figure that out?'

'Science,' he said, and disappeared off towards the kitchen.

Alice took his advice and made her way to her bedroom. She found a brush and sat down on the edge of her bed to look in the mirror on her wardrobe door. She didn't know how her hair managed to get into such a state It felt rougher than coconut matting, with knots and split ends all over the place. She wouldn't have been surprised if her father told her he'd spent the few hours she slept rubbing her head with a balloon in the hopes of making her look like a cavewoman.

Whilst she was attacking her hair, Norman brought her a mug of hot chocolate and set it on her bedside table. 'Why does Duke disagree with you about the killer?'

Alice clenched the handle of her brush tighter and wrenched it through her hair. 'Because I think that it's bleeding Clive Constable, don't I?'

'And he's Duke's friend?'

'He also happens to be in charge of the case.' Alice met her father's gaze in the mirror. 'Do you think I've got it wrong?'

'I'm not really the right person to ask.'

'Because you're my dad?'

'Because I'm an accountant.' He gave himself a moment before asking, 'Do you have any evidence that it's Clive?'

She shook her head. 'I can place his hat at the crime scene.'

He sat down on the edge of Alice's bed and handed her hot chocolate over. 'Have a drink.'

She did as he asked, sipping at it even though it still felt like lava on her tongue.

'You need evidence before you even consider accusing someone of being a murderer. That's a serious accusation, and whilst I'll support you in most things, being dozy isn't one of them. Also, he's a detective. Your evidence better be much more airtight than a bleeding hat at the crime scene.'

'They found tweed fibres on the murder weapon.

Clive's hat is tweed.'

'Do you know how many people wear tweed?'

'You don't believe me either?'

'I didn't say that. I said that you needed evidence.' Norman bit his thumbnail, thinking about something. 'I might be able to help, Al.'

'How?'

'I cycled past Arthur's the night before you found his body.'

'Did you see anyone?'

'I can't say. I was thinking more about my new helmet-cam.'

Alice's face brightened up so much, it could have been Christmas morning. 'You might have caught someone entering Arthur's house.'

He nodded. 'I've still got to transfer all the footage to my laptop. I'm finding it a bit difficult, if I'm honest. If I find anything, it could be all the help you need.'

Alice thought it was finally time to voice the worry that had been eating away at her mind for days. She said, 'What if it isn't Clive?'

'I feel sorry for whoever it is.'

'Why?'

'With you on their case, they won't know what's hit them.'

Chapter Twenty-Six

Alice called Jez and had him come to her parents' house. He arrived at the door looking startled, as though he'd been caught with a dirty magazine, but Alice didn't let that faze her. She handed over the helmet-cam and told him to get transferring and to search through the evening of Arthur's death. Jez protested, saying as it wasn't his job, at which point Alice asked him just what his job was, because so far it involved spending a lot of time breaking into her house. Needless to say, he took the helmet-cam, two pieces of apple crumble Alice had rustled up whilst she'd been waiting impatiently for him to arrive, and the knowledge he was returning home to a husband who understood the kind of crazies Jez faced on a daily basis.

She had tea with her parents – who didn't argue, remaining surprisingly amiable with one another – and returned to Falstaff Close. Only, Alice didn't return to her cottage, where she could be safe in the knowledge that someone might now be finding fresh evidence pointing towards who really killed Arthur Sterling. No, Alice parked her car outside and walked back up the road towards the scene of the crime: Arthur's cottage.

It looked normal. As normal as a cottage surrounded by crime scene tape could look. It was strange to think Arthur had only been dead for nine days. Alice felt as though her life was irrevocably changed because of her discovery. The memory of his body would forever haunt her nightmares.

When Jez first interviewed her, he'd mentioned the possibility of counsellors to help Alice through the trauma of seeing her first corpse. She'd laughed him off and didn't think it possible that a stranger's death would affect her so strongly. Yet as she crept under the crime scene tape and walked up the path towards the front door, goosepimples shocked her flesh.

Alice rubbed at her arms and inhaled through her nose, exhaled, and tried to remember all the meditation techniques Primrose had taught her, including the ones about tantric sex; at that moment in time, Alice would have accepted the deep-fried liver of a mountain goat if it offered to cure the anxiety building up in her veins, wrapping its claws around her oesophagus.

With each step it got worse, until she reached the front door, her hand around the handle, frozen to the spot.

Alice stopped stock still and stared out into the evening. A pink hue cast itself over the early summer sky. 'This isn't a horror movie, Alice,' she told herself through gritted teeth. 'There's no weirdo in a mask behind the door, waiting to grab at you.' As she spoke, she eased down the door handle, allowing it to fall open behind her.

Alice didn't allow herself to think about it any longer. She stepped backwards into Arthur's cottage and closed the door.

She didn't turn the lights on, didn't want anyone to know she was there.

Alice looked at the armchair first. Of course, his body was no longer there, but a chill still coiled its way around her spine, extending its tendrils across her ribcage, her lungs surrounded by an icy fear. Alice allowed herself the time to properly take in just how well the police had managed to clean up the place.

They hadn't been able to get all the blood out of the carpet. A dark brown mark stained the corner beside the hearth.

'This is for Arthur and Ronnie, remember that,' she said, as she took further steps into the living room. She knew the house had been searched and possible evidence taken away, but that didn't mean she wouldn't find something they'd overlooked. If they wanted to call her Miss Marple, she'd give them a blooming good reason.

Alice pulled some gloves from her pocket. She'd pilfered them from a box of hair dye that her Mum had kept in the bathroom cabinet for years – pillar box red. She'd been inspired to be more daring, but then Rihanna went and beat her to it, so she dyed her hair lilac for a month or two until someone said she looked like Mrs Slocombe and saved Alice and her father the embarrassment of having to tell her themselves.

With her gloves on, Alice began to search through the drawers and cupboards in Arthur's living room. She checked the underside of ornaments, took the backs off photograph frames, and lifted pictures to see if there was anything on the back except dust. There wasn't, but she had the devil's own job getting a landscape of Lyme Park straight on the wall afterwards.

Arthur definitely knew how to keep a secret or two.

Alice scoured every inch of the room and found nothing of any use.

She'd been about to start her search of the kitchen when she heard a car pulling up outside. Without thinking, she ran over to the back door, unlocked and opened it. Stepping onto the path, she was reminded of how these gardens were all connected, and that the flags she stood on were the escape route Arthur's murderer used.

Someone plodded up the front path. If she just turned now, she could walk down to her own garden and think nothing more of it. But Alice wanted answers, and she wouldn't find them in her own cottage, no matter how many shows she watched on Netflix. She glanced around, saw somewhere she could hide and ran over to Arthur's shed just as the front door opened.

Alice hid inside, hoping the visitor hadn't spotted her.

Arthur's shed smelled like a shed ought to smell, like creosote. Alice found herself pressed up against a lawnmower, its handle digging into her side. She looked out the rear window but saw nothing more than cobwebs and dirt. Either Arthur didn't use his shed that often or he was as filthy as the rest of the men in Partridge Mews and had been lucky enough, until nine months prior, to have a house-proud wife who didn't mind her husband having a shed that needed a trigger warning for arachnophobes.

Whoever had entered Arthur's cottage wanted to keep their presence unknown as well. Unless they came with a superhuman ability to see in the dark. The pink sky Alice had wondered at before had been replaced with the beginnings of dark blue, shadowing everything.

Alice closed her eyes in the hopes it would improve her hearing, but no matter how hard she listened, no sound came from the house – no exclamations of fury or glee, simply silence. She opened her eyes, allowing them to acclimatise once more to the grey dark of Arthur's shed, thinking that whilst she was there she might as well search the place.

She moved slowly, twisting her body around the lawnmower until she stood beside a pasting table that Arthur had wedged against the far-side of the shed. Old plant pots, paint pots and pen pots spread out across the table, connected by more cobwebs, dust and dirt. Alice searched in and around all of them, feeling as though she'd plunged her hands into a vat of candyfloss, only filthier.

She'd been about to give it up as a bad job when her hands came across it – a notebook, more of a journal than anything. Alice picked it up. It was nothing more than an A5 softcover notebook, yet her heart thundered against her ribcage as she questioned if it was Arthur's and, if so, if it contained what he'd found out about Christopher Partridge's murder.

Alice made her way back to the shed door, success bringing a smile to her face. Until she realised she was in a shed with no idea how to leave without being seen.

Unable to think of anything else, Alice pressed the door handle down slowly, inching the door open until she could slip out the slightest gap. She darted as quickly as she could to the far end of the shed, facing the gate that led out into the woods. There were similar gates in each of the gardens on Falstaff Close. They just happened to be on the other side of a stream. A trickling, burbling stream was all that stood between Alice and safety.

She jumped the short expanse and rushed to the gate, not caring for the high-pitched creak, the whine that would alert the visitor to her presence. She ran towards home. Over the squelching dirt, rocks, pebbles and overgrown foliage, until she slipped through her gate, jumped once more and sped up the path to her back door, a back door she'd made sure to lock every day since Arthur's killer used her cottage to escape.

Arthur's back door opened.

Alice flung herself to the ground and rolled onto the grass, out of sight. She hoped not being able to see whoever stood in Arthur's doorway meant that they couldn't see her. She was very aware of her loud breathing. No matter how much she tried, it still sounded as though each breath was a hoarse wheeze.

'Who's there?' he said.

Alice grimaced and stood up. 'Jez?'

He shook his head at the sight of her. 'What were you doing in Arthur's cottage?'

'Probably the same thing you were doing.'

'Searching for an intruder? One of your neighbours rang to say they'd seen someone behaving suspiciously before they broke in.'

'I was *not* behaving suspiciously.'

'You hid in the shed and then ran through the woods until you got back to your own cottage. That's behaving suspiciously.'

'How did you know?'

'I was watching through the kitchen window the entire time.' Even in the near-dark, Alice saw his smug smile.

'Before you start to gloat, can you come down and let me in? I've locked myself out.'

'Did you bother trying the handle? I've told you

much and more that the locks on these cottages are useless.'

Alice returned to the back door and tried the handle. It opened. She faced Jez once more. 'Are you coming over or what? I've found something that might be important.'

She went inside and switched on the lights, waiting for Jez.

'I thought you'd given up on being a detective,' he said when he came through the front door.

'I'm not a detective, nor did I ever claim to be.' Alice sat on the sofa, checking over her clothes. She was coated from head to toe in dust, dirt, and cobwebs. Her shoes were filthy, and she had no idea what the odour was that covered her, but she smelled as though she'd bathed in an oil drum.

'What are you, then?' Jez asked, taking a seat.

'I, like all of Partridge Mews, am a snoop.' Alice nodded in affirmation and slid the notebook across the table to him. 'I found this in Arthur's shed.'

Jez took and opened it. He read quickly, turning pages, flicking through the entire thing before he put it back down and said, 'You might have just found his notebook.'

Alice grinned. 'And they say breaking and entering is bad.'

'It is. It's illegal. You're admitting you broke the law to a police officer.'

'I did it to aid an investigation, surely that counts for something.'

Jez shook his head. 'You're the limit. You know that, don't you?'

'You know you're warming to me.'

Jez returned to looking at the notebook, rifling

through the pages, skimming them quickly. 'If you make a brew, I won't say a word.'

'Is that an officer of the law accepting bribes?'

'No, that's me getting fed up of having to make my own every time I come around.'

'Because you're forever breaking in.'

Jez winked at her. 'You know you're warming to me.'

Alice rolled her eyes and stood up. 'So much for feminism.'

Whilst she made the drinks, Jez busied himself reading through Arthur's notebook. He didn't say anything, but his eyes widened a few times.

'I'm guessing you've not had chance to look at my Dad's helmet-cam footage yet?' Alice said, returning to her seat.

Jez took his mug from her. 'I've got Ben checking it over. If he finds anything, he'll ring me.'

'How does he feel about you spending your night with a woman?'

'He's got the keys to my chastity belt, he doesn't need to worry.' He had his tongue pressed against the back of his teeth as he grinned.

'You're getting some sort of personality, Jeremy. I must be rubbing off on you.'

'I hope not.'

Alice stood and wandered over to the living room door. 'I'm going to take a shower. You'd better have found some more information by the time I'm finished.'

She went upstairs, dumping her dirty clothes outside her bedroom door.

Twenty minutes later, she returned to the living room in

her Christmas pyjamas once again. She lay down on the sofa and wrapped the throw around herself like a blanket, as though it were the deep cold of winter and not the early warning warmth of summer.

'It's getting on for June,' Jez said.

Alice shrugged. 'And there are reindeer on my pyjamas. Shall we keep pointing out the obvious, or are you going to give me Bertram Sterling's phone number?'

Jez dropped the notebook and stared at her, as unsure as a teenage boy unlocking his first bra. 'Where did that come from?'

'I thought about it just now in the shower. I could ring Bertram and ask whether he's protecting Clive.'

'I don't want to sound offensive, but that's a really stupid idea.'

'Why?'

'You didn't end things on the best of terms. He's disappeared with Flora—'

'I've absolutely no idea why the police allowed them to do that, by the way.'

'—and according to Arthur's diary, he had nothing to do with framing Ronnie.'

Alice's jaw dropped. She allowed the throw to fall away as she leant forward, planting her feet firmly on the floor. 'What do you mean?'

'There's no mention of the robbery being faked. Arthur makes it sound as though the robbery actually happened and he had to leave his post to go and help his fellow officers.'

'But everyone says Arthur got clobbered over the head, leaving him unable to identify the killer.'

Jez shook his head. 'Arthur must have been keeping some secrets of his own. Maybe this notebook, or diary, whatever it's called, is Arthur searching for his own form of forgiveness.'

'Arthur wouldn't protect Christopher's killer, would he?'

'I don't know him well enough to say, but I do know that in our reports it states that Arthur remained at Greenfields for the duration of the fete. His attack is documented.' Jez scratched the back of his head. 'I can't help but wonder if someone's trying to cover something up here.'

'We both know who was in charge back then, Jez.'

He nodded. 'I know, but it still doesn't mean we're looking at a killer.'

Chapter Twenty-Seven

Alice took the information to Duke the next morning. She hadn't felt like returning to his house but, as Jez pointed out, he might be able to shed some light on the original investigation – especially considering the contents of Arthur's notebook. Alice stood outside for as long as possible, staring at the door, looking somewhat like an over-sized garden gnome. Eventually, she plucked up the courage and knocked, a butterfly-anxiety fluttering in her chest.

He answered and fixed Alice with another look, all wide eyes and wrinkles, still ferocious. 'I wondered if you'd knock.'

'I'm not here to argue, Duke.' She handed him the notebook. 'I found this in Arthur's shed last night.'

He flicked through its pages. 'What do you expect me to do with it?'

Alice bit her tongue. She wanted to tell him to shove it where the sun doesn't shine, to force-feed the notebook to him page by page, to scream that his last remaining school-friend was a killer. But she didn't. Instead, she breathed deeply, offered what she hoped was a smile, and said, 'I found something I wanted to talk to you about.'

'That's nice, but I can't think of anything I want to talk to you about. Good day, Alice.'

He made to close the door, but Alice slammed her hand against it. 'Duke, please.'

'You need to go. Clive is on his way. We're going up to Greenfields to have a chat with Clementine. I thought it best to find someone competent to help me with the case.' With that, he closed the door, taking Arthur's notebook with him.

'He just closed the door?'

Alice nodded. 'I think he's really had it with me, Mum.'

'You did accuse his friend of murder.'

Alice went to her parents' house after her disastrous attempt at talking to Duke. At first, she rang Jez, but he was at work and had no new information for her – by the time Ben had finished downloading software to play the footage from the helmet-cam, he'd had no time to watch it before having to go to work himself.

Thus, Alice found herself driving to Wren's Lea to visit her Mum. Once again, Norman had toddled off on his bicycle, sans helmet-cam. According to Primrose, he was retracing the route he took on the night of Arthur's murder to jog his memory. She said the only memory it would jog was that of a crude display of male genitalia in tight-fitting shorts, but Alice refused to comment on that.

Instead, they took themselves into the living room, switched on ITV and muted the television so they could talk without fear of being distracted by Philip and Holly. Of course, they began with what had happened between Alice and Duke only an hour before.

Alice considered her mother's words. She realised that accusing Clive with barely-there evidence about a hat had been a bad idea, but she hadn't expected such anger from Duke. All she could think about was him bouncing ideas off Clive, when she knew he could steer the conversation towards any possible direction where he came out the hero.

'And he has the notebook,' Alice said, groaning into her Nescafé cappuccino.

'I wouldn't worry about that, love. I highly doubt the meanderings of a seventy-one-year old man are going to be accepted in court.'

'This is exactly how I got into trouble with Sylvia Cameron. Acting before I thought.'

'You're a bit like your Aunty Magdalena.'

Alice squinted at her mother. 'Where are you going with this?'

'I'm not going to say anything bad, before you get all fiercely protective. Honestly, the two of you are like bleeding bears.'

'Bears?'

'Well, I'm not sure about real bears, but the ones in the books I used to read to you.'

Alice nodded once, slowly. 'Okay.' She stretched the word out into a questioning drawl, making use of every syllable to convey the wonder at her mother's thought processes.

'Anyway, your Aunty Magdalena didn't end up with six husbands because she thought about her feelings. She married Salvador because he complimented her eyes on the French Riviera and look how well that turned out.'

'He's the one she divorced before she'd even got back to England?'

'Husband number five, I think. By then, she said she knew whether a marriage was going to work out or not, and he harboured a disdain for sticky toffee pudding that meant she had to end things.'

'And how does this relate to me and Duke?'

'Not you and Duke, but how you go about things. You've always been the same, love. If you give your ideas time to percolate and properly think about your actions before you make them, you're likely to have more success.'

'In finding murderers?'

'I just meant in general, but if that's how you want to take it, feel free.' Primrose glugged at her own drink to punctuate her sentence and grimaced. 'I'm never buying unsweetened again. I tell you, that Marcia Kennedy has some interesting ideas about food and drink, but I like my cappuccinos a bit unhealthy.'

'Is Marcia the rehabilitated vegan?'

'She says she grew tired of pretending hummus was a suitable alternative to cheddar.' Primrose stared into her mug, questioning its contents before setting it down beside the sofa. 'I might just give it to next door's cat. They like milk, don't they?'

'I'm pretty sure cats are lactose intolerant.'

'Really? But they're always drinking milk.'

'In adverts, maybe. If you feed that cat cappuccino, you're likely to come home to little brown puddles all over your back garden.'

'I'll just give it to your Dad, then.'

'You still aren't over this charity bike ride, are you?'

Primrose sighed. 'I'm not against him being charitable. I just wish he'd asked me first. And yes, that does make me something of a hypocrite after Nepal, but I did that when I was twenty-eight.'

'Have you two talked about it properly?'

'If he's not fiddling with his bike, he's spending his evenings on the laptop.' Primrose shook her head. 'Anyway, it's nothing you should worry about, love. Why don't you tell me more about the case?'

Alice shrugged. 'There's not really anything else to tell you. I accused Clive of being the murderer, now Duke isn't speaking to me and Jez says the police report shows Clive wasn't even at Greenfields when Christopher was killed.'

Her Mum squinted, before she said, 'Well that's not right.'

'What do you mean?'

'I remember seeing Clive.'

Alice allowed the words to settle, thinking over all the possible implications, before saying, 'You can't have done.'

'I might struggle to spell Oswaldtwistle but I'm not senile, Alice. Clive was there - I know he claims he wasn't, but he was there the day the heir died, and I remember full well.'

'You've got to understand it's going to be difficult to believe, considering it's taken you fifty years to realise it was vital information.'

'I didn't know it was vital information, did I? I was five years old, in desperate need of the lavatory. I asked him where it was, and he pointed me in the right direction. I wasn't about to ask him if he planned to go and nobble his cousin.'

'I know. It's given me something else to be going on with.'

'You never know, it might help you in the long run, love.'

Alice nodded, unable to deny the tension in her

chest. If Jez found anything in the helmet-cam footage, then she might just be on her way to finding a killer.

Chapter Twenty-Eight

There was no sign of anybody in the helmet-cam footage. Jez returned her Dad's equipment later that day, saying most of the time her father was looking down, leading to some shots that left both Jez and his husband feeling uncomfortable.

Alice and Primrose were in the kitchen. They'd planned on making some sort of salad with the halloumi that Primrose had bought but had no idea how to use. Once they'd found their way from the living room to the kitchen, they ended up sitting at the counter and sharing a box of Ferrero Rocher they'd stashed beneath the sink.

They offered one to Jez as he sat himself down. 'Thanks,' he said, accepting the offer.

'What do you do now?' Primrose asked.

Alice looked to Jez for an answer, but he wouldn't speak with his mouth full so she was left to reply, 'I have absolutely no idea.'

'That sounds a bit pessimistic, love.'

Jez nodded. 'You're right, Mrs Valentine.'

Alice stuck her tongue out at Jez. 'All right, since you're the detective, what are your ideas?'

'We couldn't find anything on the helmet-cam footage, but what about dash-cams? There are tons of them around.'

'And you think someone might have nipped down Falstaff Close for the joy of filming it?' Alice rolled her eyes. 'Thanks, Jez, but I'm not sure there are enough anoraks in the world.'

'Just to play devil's advocate,' Primrose said. 'Your Dad did go down there and record. I'm sure there's more than just him recording their every route through traffic.'

'Are we all planning on ganging up on me today?'

'Get on Facebook and search Partridge Mews dash cam,' Jez said. 'You'll be surprised.'

Alice did as he said and shook her head. 'I can't believe it.'

She scrolled through a group on Facebook, astounded by the number of people in town who'd recorded their every journey and uploaded it, adding captions about the daily commute or the latest trip to the supermarket. An entire tribe of dull troglodytes had found their way online and discovered an innovative new way to bore their peers.

'Do you want to keep searching or shall I show you what I found?' Jez asked, a slim smile on his face.

Alice set her phone on the counter and glared at him. 'Are you honestly saying you've been sitting there all this time with the footage we've been looking for?'

His smile fell. 'Well, I thought—'

'Mum, hit him around the head for me.'

'You know I don't condone violence, love.'

'Fine.' Alice leaned over and clouted Jez. 'Don't be such an idiot next time.'

He rubbed at his ear. 'I could have you done for

assaulting an officer.'

'Do it. I'll tell them you were withholding evidence.'

'It's a freely available video that I'm about to share with a friend. Try it.'

'Will you pair give it a rest? Jez, whilst I agree it was a bit absent-minded to not mention you'd found footage related to the murder, considering my daughter has a flair for the dramatic, I can't see she has any room to talk.' Primrose stared them both down.

Jez glanced across at Alice. 'Is she always like this?'

'Motherly?' Alice nodded. 'If she went on Mastermind, her specialist subject would be parenting manuals of the twenty-first century.'

'Good to know.'

'Will you please show us the video?' Primrose asked.

Jez took out his phone and balanced it in front of the Ferrero Rocher box so they could all watch the video. He pressed play and they all watched as the car threaded through the streets of Partridge Mews. The driver allowed a car to turn into Falstaff Close and then followed them. By the time they'd pulled into the road, the other car had pulled up outside Arthur's cottage.

Alice watched with bated breath as Detective Inspector Clive Constable climbed out of his car. 'I knew it,' she exclaimed.

Jez paused the video and returned his phone to his pocket. 'I'd like to point out that this doesn't prove anything besides the fact he was there on the night of Arthur's death.'

'Even so, that would make him the last person to see Arthur alive. Why hasn't he mentioned that beforehand? He claims he was nowhere near Greenfields when Christopher was killed, but my Mum saw him.'

Jez glanced at Primrose. 'Is this true?'

'I needed the loo and my Mum said as there were enough toilets in the Hall. Officially, we weren't supposed to go inside, but she said they could handle the bladder urgency of a five-year-old. That's when I saw Clive.'

Alice recalled waiting for Duke and the police to arrive after finding Arthur's body, how Clive came running up the hill from the direction of her cottage, hair flailing about all over the place, and the look of concern on Jez's face. 'Clive shouldn't have been there,' she said. 'He shouldn't have been at Greenfields, and he shouldn't have been at Arthur's, but he was in both places.'

'What are you thinking?'

'Where's Clive's car? He didn't just run all the way from the station when he heard about Arthur. And why's he coming uphill? If he's coming from the direction of town, he'd be heading down towards Arthur's.

'What if I interrupted him? You all say Ronnie was killed elsewhere and that his body was moved. What if he went to Arthur's and found Clive stood over the body? They row, and Clive kills him as well, but I arrive, and Clive ends up hiding himself and Ronnie.'

'Don't you think you would have seen him?'

'My focus was entirely on the corpse I'd just found. I didn't go around checking if there was anyone in the house who might be able to give me more information.'

'Do you think he's the one who hid the murder weapon in your cottage?'

'I think he saw me and hid. When I came outside, he hid Ronnie's body as best he could, then ran down to my cottage where he stashed the murder weapon before running up the hill to meet us. None of us would have expected a detective – and Arthur's friend – to be his killer. We wouldn't question the direction he came in.'

'Or his lack of vehicle,' Primrose said.

Alice willed Jez to believe her. It all fit. She felt it in the marrow of her bones, the hair sticking up on the back of her neck and the gooseflesh prickling along her arms and legs. Clive Constable had killed Arthur Sterling.

Eventually, Jez conceded with a nod. 'We've got barely any evidence if I report this, Alice. All our hopes lie in the notebook. Where is it?'

Alice's heart dropped into her stomach. 'Duke took it.'

'All right. Whilst that may be a problem, I'll go around and ask for it back. He won't say no to an officer of the law.'

'That's not the issue, Jez. Duke said Clive was going to take him to Greenfields. What if he's seen the notebook and thinks Duke has read it? He's already killed three times, I doubt he'll mind a fourth.'

'I'll ring it in,' he said.

'You'll do more than that, Jeremy Carson. You're taking me to Greenfields now. I'm not having another death on my conscience.'

Chapter Twenty-Nine

Jez drove a lot faster than he ought to have done. Alice had to admit she was impressed, even if she was slightly afraid for her life. He might have been spurred on by her constantly nagging at him and complaining that they weren't going to get there in time, and that Clive would end up covering up another murder, which would in turn lead to him killing them. Just a few simple words of encouragement to really give him the full picture of the situation.

Primrose had wanted to come along as well, but Alice forced her to stay home. Alice had her reasons for not wanting her mother there, the main one being that Primrose didn't care for violence and Alice couldn't promise she wouldn't leather someone if anything happened to Duke.

Their journey drew to a halt when a farmer decided it was the perfect time to allow his cows to cross the road. Jez cursed under his breath and drummed his fingers against the steering wheel.

'I think I deserve a Pinot Grigio,' Alice said whilst they waited.

'Why's that?' Jez asked, so restless that the words

practically buzzed from his lips.

'Because I'm about to go and save the life of Marmaduke Featherstone. Only a few weeks ago, I wouldn't have cared either way what happened to him. Now look at me. Despite him being a complete idiot, I'm going to help him.' She grinned, looking smug. Sure, there was a definite restlessness that Alice felt in her core, that if the cows didn't move fast enough she might just get out and make some fresh burgers where they stood, but she was trying to suppress that with breathing exercises and the idea that Duke would be able to talk himself out of the situation.

'You realise Duke wouldn't even be with Clive if you'd kept your mouth shut?'

Alice pressed her tongue against the back of her teeth and breathed deep through her nose. 'Yes, I realise that. It's one of the many completely selfish reasons I have to save his life.'

Jez leaned his head against his window. 'You're not to blame for any of these deaths, you know, Alice.'

She nodded but couldn't allow herself to think about Arthur or Ronnie, because if she did she knew that the guilt in her stomach would rise like bile and tears would burst free from her eyes like Niagara Falls in a monsoon. 'Let's just get to Duke,' she said.

'There's every chance he's okay. We're going because we've decided that Clive is a killer. He might not be. He and Duke could be inside with Clementine, enjoying cups of tea and those horrible cakes you told me about.'

Alice heaved another deep breath that sent her teeth chattering. 'Thanks for trying, but we both know I'm right.'

When the last cow entered the field, Jez drove off

down the road, hitting speeds that probably shouldn't have been attempted on country roads.

They didn't make it to Greenfields.

Alice yelled, 'Wait!'

Jez screeched the car to a halt. 'What did you make me do that for?'

She pointed behind them at an old beige Audi which was pulled up on a grass verge. 'Isn't that Clive's car?'

Jez checked his mirrors, forever diligent, and reversed back down the road until they were adjacent with the other vehicle. He ballooned his cheeks and hissed a breath. 'That's Clive's, all right. I really think I have to phone this in, Alice.'

But she was already out of the car, the door slammed behind her.

Clive had tried to hide his car beneath the canopy of the trees, parking as close to the white metal fence as possible without scraping his paintwork. He must have climbed over the railings alongside Duke and led him into the depths of Greenfields Woods.

Alice looked through the driver's window – Arthur's notebook was on the passenger seat. She tried the handle, but the door was locked.

Jez parked his car further down the road and came running back to her. 'There's no reception up here, Alice. We need to drive to the house and use their phone, contact the proper people for help.'

Alice had her hands against the bonnet. 'The engine's still hot. They might not have been gone that long.'

She didn't bother waiting for an answer from Jez.

Alice crossed the grass verge and climbed over the fence into the woods. The ground was soft underfoot; bark and stray twigs cracked beneath her soles. She inhaled the scent of wild garlic and mulch, green smells that reminded her of days spent foraging with Aunty Magdalena.

Jez followed her. 'If there's any trouble, you might as well have an officer on your side.'

'There are certain things that police officers aren't allowed to do when they find a killer, Jez.'

'Like what?'

'I'm going to rip that lying tongue right out of his head,' she said, her words certain, more of a lioness's growl than mere speech.

He winced. 'You know, you really shouldn't tell me that sort of thing.'

'Why ask, then?'

Alice scrutinised the ground, searching for footprints, a track they might have taken. Once she was certain which way they should go, she started walking.

These woods held fond memories for almost everyone in Partridge Mews and the surrounding areas. As kids, Alice and her friends would meet up with bottles of whatever cheap alcohol their parents wouldn't miss. They'd sample cigarettes, share tentative first kisses no one ever need know about and then tell everyone anyway. She remembered a night spent camping in the woods, how they awoke in the morning to find a family of deer parading past them, as though reminding them this was their forest and that Alice and her friends were merely guests.

Now, Alice wandered through the woods to catch a murderer, stopping occasionally to check she could still see footprints in the mud, broken twigs crunched beneath heavy feet. Clearly, she'd learned a thing or two from her Aunty Magdalena, besides where best to find mushrooms that could induce vomiting – but that one had been after Isaac Leadbetter dumped her for Chloe Hall in year ten.

After they'd been walking for a quarter of an hour, Alice stopped in her tracks. She faced Jez and held a finger to her lips. She'd heard something within the trees, the sound of indistinct raised voices, but no matter how much she strained to listen, she couldn't tell what was being said.

'I think we need to go this way,' Jez said, pointing to the left.

Alice smiled and nodded. Someone had stepped off the path, crushing bushes and other foliage beneath their feet.

They made their way over, moving as quietly as they could, lifting their legs comically high to avoid making even the slightest rustle. They reached a small clearing and hid behind a tree, because Clive had a shotgun and he had it aimed directly at Duke's chest.

'What do we do?' Alice whispered.

He handed her his keys. 'Go back to the car and head to the Hall. Ring the police.'

'Sod that.' She thrust his keys back at him.

Alice stepped out from behind the tree and stormed into the clearing.

'Alice?' Duke said.

'Are you planning on putting that gun down soon or do you want to wait until your colleagues get here?' Alice glowered at Clive, pressing her nails into her palms in the hope it would hide the fear in her chest.

Clive returned her glare and said, 'How about I shoot you as well?'

Alice couldn't help herself, she rolled her eyes. 'You're serious, aren't you? You're actually serious.' She faced Duke. 'Can you believe he's serious?'

Duke looked at her warily, as though he thought she'd finally flipped her lid.

She returned her gaze to Clive. 'You're a murderer, you idiot. You've killed three people. Everybody knows. Killing another two isn't going to change that.'

His face fell, lips trembling. 'What do you mean?'

'You're smarter than this, mantis-man. I wasn't about to drive all the way here without getting in touch with the police first. Oh, I just happen to know where a murderer is, and I'm going to go and confront him with no help.'

'You're bluffing,' he said. 'They wouldn't believe you.'

Alice leaned against a tree and yawned. 'All right. Your hat was bathing in Arthur's blood, there's a video of you going into his house on the night of his death, and I'm pretty sure if we checked your shoes, they'd match the footprints left all over my kitchen floor.'

'All of that is circumstantial.'

'You're standing in the woods with a gun aimed at somebody. How exactly are you going to explain that one?'

Clive looked from the shotgun to Duke and back as though he'd forgotten they were there. He cocked the gun over his arm, cradling it over his elbow. 'Why couldn't you all just leave it well alone?'

'Do you know, Clive, I really am beginning to believe you're a bit of an idiot.'

'Alice,' Duke warned.

'No, Duke. This man over here killed one of his closest friends and an innocent man simply because they figured out he murdered his cousin.'

'He was having an affair!' Clive yelled. His voice broke as though he was on the verge of tears, panic filling his every pore. In that moment, Alice saw a teenager again, a young boy with a clear idea of right and wrong.

'You're talking about Ronnie, aren't you?'

Her words stopped him in his tracks. He'd been all set to protest something, to share another insult or accusation. Instead, he said, 'How do you know about Ronnie?'

'Because Clementine told us. She knew Christopher and Ronnie were in a relationship before they married, that theirs had been a marriage of convenience.' Alice shrugged. 'She told us you knew all about the relationship and were keeping it a secret.'

Clive looked incredulous – it was in the arch of his brow and the taut clench of his fingers. 'I thought she knew he was having an affair. I didn't know she knew who with.'

'She knew,' Duke affirmed. 'Called it the purest love she'd seen.'

'I've been protecting her for fifty years and she *knew*?' Clive roared, the words strong enough to tear his vocal cords in half.

'Clive, what are you saying, lad?' Duke edged his way towards his friend.

'Why else do you think I killed Christopher? What he and Ronnie were doing. I thought it was all behind her back, but, no, she was letting it all happen.' He traipsed back and forth across the clearing, his eyes darting this way and that.

'You planned to frame Ronnie for the murder, didn't you?'

'Know all about that, do you?'

'Bertram Sterling told us there was a group of you. That he faked the armed robbery to stop Ronnie being framed.'

Clive laughed, he actually chuckled, as he stood there. 'That's right. Bloody Bertie's little fondness for Ronnie Butterworth. Worked out in the end though, didn't it?'

'What do you mean?' This came from Alice, who was still hoping that Clive might forget all about his gun. She also wondered just where Jez had got to – she hadn't heard any rustling behind her, but if he was still hiding behind a tree, she might just throttle him.

She didn't have much time to think about it though, because Clive had more of his tale to tell. 'Bertram hadn't banked on Arthur leaving his post. Arthur arrived at the jewellers after everyone else had left. When my father arrived back at Greenfields, he found Christopher had been killed and Arthur was nowhere to be seen.

'Turns out Arthur saw something he shouldn't have done, and my father was only too happy to say Arthur had been attacked as well, so long as Arthur said nothing about Christopher and Ronnie having at it in the drawing room.'

'I'm guessing you're the one who summoned Ronnie to Greenfields that day?' Duke asked. He looked unsure of himself, his eyes darting between Clive, Alice, and the gun.

Clive shook his head. 'No, but I'm the one who asked him inside. He went to see Christopher, but there was some disturbance outside. Ronnie went to investigate and whilst he was out, I grabbed that damn dog off the mantelpiece and bashed Christopher over the head with it, again, and again.'

Alice grimaced, images of Arthur's body flashing through her mind, practically imprinted on her eyelashes. 'You wanted to make a proper job of it?'

'Exactly.'

'And nobody ever thought it could be you?'

'As far as my father was concerned, I was in another squad car, being patiently ferried around Partridge Mews.'

'But you weren't?'

'I told the young copper who should've been looking after me that I'd nipped off to have my way with Margery Inman behind the cricket pavilion. He actually bought me half a shandy on the promise that I wouldn't tell my father he'd lost me, and he wouldn't tell him I might have got some poor lass in trouble.' Clive had a smirk on his face the likes of which would have impressed many a Disney villain.

Alice felt sick to her stomach. Here she was, faced with a murderer, and he didn't show even an ounce of remorse, no regret over his actions, simply pride over a job well done.

'And that was it. For fifty years, nobody bothered to figure out what happened at the fete. Until Arthur's wife died.'

'He couldn't leave it well alone. Everything worked out fine. Clementine inherited the estate upon my uncle's death, and we rarely spoke of Christopher. And then Arthur started poking his nose in again.'

'It wasn't just Arthur though, was it?' Duke said. He stepped towards Clive, his eyes as wide as a hawk's, all set to devour its prey. 'Because Ronnie had started asking questions as well. Folk around town never trusted him again and he wanted to clear his name.'

'That's not all,' Alice added, 'because Clementine had also started redeveloping the west wing, and that's where you were hiding the murder weapon.'

'I'd never kill Clem. She's my sister. Besides, if anyone had stumbled across the Jack Russell, they'd only have a murder weapon. They'd have no idea who had used it.'

'Is that why you became a detective? To make sure no one ever found out about your crime?'

'No, you idiot. It was to continue my father's legacy. He was in the force, so I joined the force. It was nothing to do with covering my tracks. I had no need. Truth be told, I never thought anyone would find out.'

'So how did Arthur find out?' Duke asked.

'Because Bertram got guilty, didn't he? Back in the day, we kept him quiet because we threatened to tell everyone about how he fancied boys. Then it became easy because he faked the robbery and framed Ronnie.'

Duke scratched at his head before saying, 'Bertie tells Arthur, then Arthur comes to you? For what? Why didn't he just let the proper authorities know?'

'He wanted to give me the opportunity to do the right thing. I'm due to retire soon, and for some unfathomable reason, he actually believed I'd want my final days on the force to be compromised by a mistake I made as a teenager. He expected they'd be lenient, but I wasn't about to take my chances.

'That evening, when I went around, he confronted me with the Jack Russell from Greenfields. Clementine had allowed him a look at the west wing, and he'd brought it along, hoping the shock would cause me to confess. I did. I confessed my sins as I cracked his skull in two.'

'Why did you go back?' Alice asked.

'I'm not sure what you're talking about.' The corpse-like grin still hadn't left his face, serving to unnerve Alice even further.

As she heard the faint sound of sirens in the distance, she said, 'The next morning you went back and killed Ronnie.'

'Oh, that? I didn't go back to kill Ronnie. I went to clean the place up. The night before, I had to get home to Helena. She's always made such a fuss about my work-life balance. Anyway, I get back to the cottage as Ronnie is going inside. Those locks really are notoriously bad. I'd get yours sorted, if I were you.

'Ronnie finds Arthur's body, and when I walk in he puts two and two together. Before I had a chance to say anything, he was screaming at me. I hit him just to shut him up. I realised how bad it looked so I hid his body in the garden shed and collected it that night.'

'You must have known someone would realise he died from a cracked skull and not from hanging?'

Clive nodded. 'I thought I might as well give it a shot. I planned to lean on the coroner and ask them to rule it as a suicide to make the investigation a bit easier. He's had a few issues of malpractice I'm sure he wouldn't want folk knowing about.'

'You're quite good at blackmail, aren't you?'

He grinned at her, a broad grin, looking every inch the Cheshire Cat as he sauntered towards her with the gun over his arm. 'It's the way of the world, Alice. The sooner you catch on, the better.'

She wasn't sure why she did what she did next, only that an anger unlike anything she'd ever felt before overcame her. Fury rushed throughout her body and, without thinking, Alice punched Clive.

He crumpled to the ground, dropping his shotgun, and Alice wondered at the solidity of Clive's cheekbones because her knuckles felt as though they'd just been attacked by concrete.

Clive remained on the ground, amongst the leaves and soil, until the police arrived, led by Jez.

'I want her arrested for assaulting an officer,' Clive said, pointing at the large red welt beginning to bloom on his face. His colleagues led him away, refusing to talk to him as they headed back towards Greenfields Hall.

Duke looked from the officers to Alice, indecision etched into every wrinkle.

'Go, Duke. We can talk later,' she said.

Jez walked towards her, his face a picture of astonishment.

'You went back for the car, then?' Alice said, a smile on her face.

'Not everyone can go launching themselves at an old man with a shotgun.'

'Especially not married men. What would Ben say if he found out you'd jumped at the first chance of another man's barrel?'

'You'll have to come to tea one evening and find out.'

Alice considered it for a moment. 'All right then, but I'll supply dessert. How does he feel about beetroot?'

Chapter Thirty

'Truth be told, I knew you were right when you mentioned the hat.'

'I know.'

'I thought you might.'

'He was your friend, Duke. I shouldn't have just blurted out he was a killer.' They were sitting in Alice's living room. When Duke didn't arrive immediately following Clive's arrest, she worried they were back to square one, with one of them being too embarrassed to speak to the other.

That morning, spurred on by too much Kenco before 10AM, Alice telephoned Duke and said, 'You've not been around, Duke. Haven't got cold feet, have you?'

'Alice? I–'

'Only we've solved a murder, and I don't bake cakes for just anybody.'

There'd been some reluctance to leave his pit – she still found herself surprised by how much the man could sleep – before Alice finally convinced Duke to come round and sort things out between them.

It had been a few days since Clive's arrest, and

despite regular updates from Jez, Alice didn't know much more than that Clive had finally confessed to his crimes and had subsequently been charged with the murders of Christopher Partridge, Arthur Sterling and Ronnie Butterworth. Now, as with many of his cases, Jez found himself buried beneath a mountain of paperwork. And, as such, Alice was left alone in her cottage.

She made a Victoria sponge because it was early summer, and she felt her inner Mary Berry rising to the surface. The cake was filled with enough cream to make a Weight Watcher abandon their salad; thick waves of jam swirled over the thick sponge, and she'd also dotted fresh strawberries across the surface of the cake because she didn't care about archaic rules as to what made a traditional Victoria sponge. 'This is an Alice sponge,' she'd announced as she finished decorating it, though there'd been no one around to hear her.

Alice had to admit that she still felt some grief surrounding the cottage. Sometimes it felt as though it could never be hers, that Aunty Magdalena's presence was what made Alice feel at home in the first place and that without her it was simply the building in which she chose to live. She wondered if any of the changes she was making – the new wallpaper, still in its wrapper against the wall, or the furnishings she hadn't yet purchased – would make the cottage feel like hers, or if the memories of life with Aunty Magdalena would always get in the way.

In the end, she resigned herself to simply not knowing the future. It might not have been a perfect answer, but it was all she had to be going on with.

She also had Duke, a man who had his own grief – grief for his missing niece and the friends he'd lost. She supposed they'd have to figure things out between them.

Alice cut herself and Duke two large slabs of cake to have with their mugs of tea. It didn't feel like a china cup day.

'You saved my life,' he said. 'After all I said, you still saved my life.'

Alice nodded. 'I mean, I did consider leaving you there, but I didn't really fancy seeing a third dead man in as many weeks.'

Duke looked down at his plate in response, his skin still a little pale, his cheeks as droopy as a bloodhound with the jowls of John Major.

'Anyway, Duke,' she said. 'We don't have to sit here making apologies. We know by now what we're like. We're going to argue, I might throw a few things, then we'll calm down and get over it. It's all part of a healthy friendship. If we say sorry every time, we'll just be wasting breath.'

Here was a man who didn't mind talking with his mouth full, sloshing bits of sponge and jam and cream around his mouth like a cement mixer, with sound effects as well. 'Ah, I suppose you're right. Are they going to be prosecuting you for assaulting Clive?'

Alice shrugged. 'They can try. You find a court in this land which will support a lecherous old murderer over a young woman.'

'He's a former detective, and he would've been an OAP.'

'It's in the papers. I'm renowned for my disrespect towards the older generation. He should have known he had it coming.'

They grinned at one another as Duke said, 'Now you're getting it.'

Alice allowed their smiles to die down before mentioning something she wanted to get out in the open so they could move forward with no secrets. 'I know about Joanna,' she said.

Duke looked lost for words, so Alice sliced him another sliver of cake. Once he regained his power of speech, through the smacking of his lips and a few sips of hot tea, he said, 'That'll be Primrose, I expect?'

Alice nodded. 'The last time we fell out, I mentioned the photos in your house. She told me about Joanna.'

'You better not be thinking of going all sympathetic. Is that why you made the cake?'

'I made the cake because I've been stuck in this house for three days with little else to do. I doubt I could become sympathetic with you if I tried. You've as much need for sympathy as a goat has for stilettos.'

He nodded and attacked the extra piece of cake she gave him. 'Why'd you bring it up, then?'

'There are no secrets between us, and I thought I could help you try and find her.'

'Got the investigating bug, have you? Think you've managed to solve one historical case, you might as well try your hands at solving another?'

Alice nodded. 'You're right on both counts, but there's one other reason.'

'What's that?'

'I really want to get your house tidy.'

He looked at her gone out. 'I thought you were meant to be a modern woman or something. All feminism and no vacuuming.'

'Technically, I've been something of a freelance detective these last few weeks, using your house as my workplace. Therefore, my workplace is in breach of health and safety laws, and as such I'm asking my employer, you, to fix said breaches.'

'No need to look so smug. How long have you been thinking about this?'

'Since I found you sprawled out on a bed of bin liners and thought you were dead. Your house is one of the most serious cases of hoarding I've ever witnessed, and I once had to visit a woman who kept bottle caps going back to 1962.'

He gave her an enquiring look.

'She made necklaces.' Alice cocked her head to the side. 'So, what do you say? Can I help you find your niece?'

Duke handed her his plate and said, 'It couldn't hurt, could it? Now, what do you say to another slice of cake to seal the deal?'

Alice rolled her eyes. 'Fine, but I saved your life, Marmaduke Featherstone. You owe me a Pinot Grigio.'

Alice took the rest of the cake to her parents'. Norman said he had something he wanted to share with both Alice and Primrose that evening.

'What do you think it is?' Alice asked.

'I've no idea, love. We're still not on the best of terms, though he did give me a kiss goodbye this morning.'

'Doesn't he always do that?'

'Yes, but this morning I actually let him.'

Once again, they found themselves sat at the kitchen counter. Primrose had found a new green tea at the wholefoods shop that she wanted to try, and apparently she also wanted to watch it for all of its two-minute steeping time.

Alice settled for a glass of water. She'd grown tired of all the tea and coffee constantly being sent her way and thought her bladder might be grateful for the lack of caffeine.

'I imagine you're quite glad it turned out Clive was the killer,' Primrose said, staring into her cup. She'd used her glass mug so she could properly see the colour of her tea change.

'I wouldn't say I'm glad, Mum. There are still three dead men because of him. Bertram Sterling's left town. Clive's caused a lot of damage.'

'I'm happy he won't be around to cause any more harm.'

An alarm on Primrose's phone went off and she lifted the teabag from her cup by its string, squeezed it a few times between thumb and forefinger, wincing, and dropped it into the bin, as precise with her movements as a surgeon over an appendectomy.

'I've said I'm going to help Duke find Joanna.'

Primrose lifted her cup to her nose and inhaled. 'I thought you might.'

'Really?'

'Honestly, love, why else do you think I told you? It'll do you and Duke good to work together.'

'We just have. He nearly ended up dead.'

'But he didn't, because you showed up. I'm telling you, it'll be a dream partnership. Eventually.' Primrose took a sip of her green tea and recoiled, her face contorting as though she'd just licked a toad.

'Too hot?' Alice asked.

'One of the great pleasures of green tea,' Primrose said, 'is that it often reminds you of the pains one must go to for their health.' She grabbed the honey off the counter and poured a dessertspoonful into her mug.

'Doesn't the honey eliminate all the health benefits?'

'It's a sacrifice I'm willing to make.' Primrose

nodded and took another sip. 'Much better.'

Alice grinned at her Mum, shaking her head.

The front door opened, and Norman called to them as he wandered down the hall into the kitchen. 'I thought you'd be in here,' he said. 'How are you doing, Alice?'

'I found a killer, stopped him doing it again, and baked a cake. I think I'm doing all right.'

'I'm sorry about the footage from my helmet-cam.'

Alice nodded. 'So am I. Honestly, Dad, how would you feel if your friends ended up watching a video that was nothing more than close-up shots of your father's crotch?'

He gulped. 'Fair point.'

'Sex mad, that's your problem, love,' Primrose said, hiding a filthy grin behind her mug.

'That must be it. Anyway, do you want to know what your surprise is?' He could barely contain his excitement. It was practically an electrical energy buzzing off him, in the lift of his shoulders and the near bouncing on the spot as he grinned at the two of them.

'We'd best go now, Mum. He looks fit to explode.'

'And I could do without that all over my kitchen.'

Alice and Primrose stood and followed Norman out of the house. 'Close your eyes,' he said, leaving them on the doorstep as he scuttled down the front path.

They did as he asked. Alice heard the whine of the gate and the slight rattle of a sound she'd grown to associate with her father – the sound of a bicycle chain, or rather, of two bicycle chains. 'He hasn't, has he?' Primrose murmured.

'I hope not.'

'You can open your eyes now.'

They opened their eyes to find Norman standing in

the middle of the road, a broad smile on his face, holding his handlebars. Alice couldn't believe the gleaming paintwork of the very new, and very expensive…

'Tandem?' Primrose exclaimed. 'You bought a tandem?'

Norman's smile wavered somewhat, but he maintained it. 'I know you're a bit upset about me going off on this charity bike ride, and I realised that I'd miss you too, and the best way to combat that would be for us to go together. So I searched all over the place, in shops, supermarkets, and online, and eventually I found her. We can do this bike ride together, Prim. What do you say?'

Alice watched as the tears brimmed in her mother's eyes. A smile trembled on her lips as she made her way towards Norman and embraced him, wrapping her arms around his neck. 'You've got to be one of the most thoughtful men I know, Norman Valentine.'

'It's all your doing, love. What do you say we take her for a spin?'

'But only to the end of the road and back,' Alice said. 'I'm friendly with the local constabulary now. I don't want any reports of my parents stopping for afternoon delight in the bushes.'

Her parents sat on the tandem and set off shakily down the road, winding this way and that between the parked cars. Their neighbours came out to watch them as Norman talked her through what to do and Primrose squealed in delight.

A subtle warmth that was common for the beginning of summer surrounded them as the sky regained its pink hues. The air was thick with pollen, the promise of new beginnings, where bees and butterflies could flit between flowers to their heart's content.

Norman and Primrose reached the end of the street and rode back towards Alice, laughing like young lovers. They dismounted and walked up the garden path, arms wrapped around each other, sharing well-wishes with those who'd come outside to watch them.

Alice stood in the doorway, watching her parents with a grin on her face that she hoped would never subside.

Sure, she'd lost her job, been involved in a fifty-year-old murder investigation, helped to catch a killer and rediscovered an old friend, but it was moments like these that made her appreciate all that she had. As her parents approached her, she had only one question upon her lips.

'Who's for cake?' she asked.

Acknowledgements

Oftentimes, we hear that it takes a village to get a book ready for publication. Such is the case with *An Heir to Murder*.

This book wouldn't be in your hands had it not been for the help I received from several people. There are not enough words to express my gratitude, so a few of them will have to do.

Cathryn Heathcote, Margaret Holbrook, Lindsey Watson and Joy Winkler read this book before anyone else. They critiqued, advised, and I couldn't have asked for better support.

Booktube helped me find an editor in the form of Dane Cobain. I am forever grateful for the work you put in to polishing this book and for pointing out when I was being too northern.

I kept Alice's story secret for the longest time, because I didn't know how she'd be received, so I want to thank you, the reader, for giving her a chance.

For those of you who have been here since the beginning, until next time, that is all.

Printed in Poland
by Amazon Fulfillment
Poland Sp. z o.o., Wrocław